VETTED FOR Violence

TYLER RHODES

Copyright © 2024 Tyler Rhodes

This is a work of fiction. Names, characters, businesses, places, events and incidents are either the products of the author's imagination or used in a fictitious manner. Any resemblance to actual persons, living or dead, or actual events is purely coincidental.

.

Dedicated to all the dog owners. Life just isn't the same without a muddy buddy messing up the sofa and barking at penguins on the TV! (Or is that just ours?)

Chapter 1

"Hang in there, Anxious," I soothed as my petrified Jack Russell Terrier whined pitifully from the passenger seat. "We'll be there soon, and the, er, doctor will make you feel better. You just have a poorly paw, but you're a brave boy. That's it, keep holding it up, and it's not so bad. Nothing but a little scratch."

Vee, my 1967 VW split-screen campervan, juddered again as I tried to increase speed, but the old girl was having none of it and refused to do as she was supposed to. I dropped into third, hoping it might improve things, but as I shifted the large gearstick, more like something you'd expect on a bus than a small camper, I crunched it horribly and the entire vehicle shuddered as though I'd slammed on the brakes. Then we sailed forward, free and smooth, and I sighed with relief as I accelerated.

With his paw held aloft, Anxious whimpered. His white fur with cute brown patches bristled as he trembled. His eyes widened as he glanced from the bloody gash revealing pink flesh to me, mournful and yet full of hope that I would make him better. I wanted to hug him, maybe shed a tear, but I had to remain strong for him, and I had to get us to the vets as fast as possible.

I was trying my best, willing Vee to go faster, but there was definitely something wrong with my home on wheels. I was as much a mechanic as I was an astronaut, and would most likely fare better in space than underneath the antique vehicle with a spanner.

As we trundled along a quiet road, with the sun beating down ferociously amidst the continuing heatwave that the weather people promised would last all summer, I felt no cheer. Our vanlife had been going so well, and we'd done nothing but relax after the pickle at the pub, and boy had we needed it. It had been perfect, with one-pot cooking every night, a few delightful campsites in the heart of Wales, long walks in the countryside, and plenty of dozing under the sun shelter.

Now here we were approaching Harlech on the north-west coast of Wales, but things had gone horrendously wrong. Vee had been playing up, unresponsive to gear changes and losing power, and I was headed to a garage not far from the historic town when everything went pear-shaped. A quick nip into the bushes for a much-needed pee for us both had resulted in Anxious howling in pain and me rapidly zipping up my jeans to find that he'd caught his paw in a tin can some muppet had left along with a bag of rubbish rather than keeping their trash in their vehicle. Why on earth would you litter like that? I'd freed his foot as he sat there trembling, and now we were closing in on a veterinary clinic I'd already called to confirm they could see us.

A car passed us, the driver beeping his smug horn and pointing as he sailed by. I glanced in the rearview mirror to find smoke belching from the exhaust, and then the campervan spasmed again, causing my stress levels to skyrocket as Anxious howled in fear and slumped down onto the seat then put his paws over his ears.

"Nearly there, buddy. You're being such a brave boy. The vet... er, the doctor will probably give you a sticker for coping so well." I glanced over to check if he'd heard me say the V word, but seemingly I'd got away with it. There were two things in this world that Anxious hated: vets and rabbits. One he chased after, the other he ran away from.

With the engine taking a break from whatever ailed it, and the road ahead clear, I focused on my driving and navigated the twists and turns of a typical Welsh road where all the signs were in both Welsh and English, roadworks signs and temporary traffic light installations seemed to be a national pastime—although I never saw any actual work being carried out—and the speed limits varied between fifty and twenty for no apparent reason and with frustrating regularity.

I spied the Irish Sea between dense rhododendrons as we emerged from the shade of a narrow stretch of spindly trees, the dazzlingly blue water and sky making it impossible to tell where one ended and the other began. Boats bobbed lazily, ushering forth visions of days lounging around being served cocktails, and I thought I spied Harlech Castle before we were enveloped in the strange twilight world once more.

Then I took a bend and we were clear of the cloying, shadow world and immersed in the pure glory of a perfect summer's day with the rugged coastline stretching east to west. I followed the route on my phone and passed rows of bungalows where gardens brimmed with hydrangeas in gaudy pastel shades, bursting with life, then took a side road past regimented green holiday homes, on to a peaceful residential street, then climbed up the side of a hill before spying the clinic up ahead.

"One more minute, then we'll be there. Stay strong."

Anxious shuffled about on the seat, whimpering as he put pressure on his foot, then he sat and stared first at me then out of the split-screen at the nice grounds surrounding the clinic. It must have been a boarding kennels as well, because the well-manicured grounds were expansive and very pretty with borders brimming with dazzling plants, picnic benches with people drinking coffees, and a large car park. A woman in green scrubs was walking five dogs; three others ran loose and having tremendous fun.

Belching smoke, and with the vehicle stuttering and starting, I crawled into the car park, yanked on the handbrake, and with a grateful sigh I killed the engine.

Wasting no time, I unbuckled Anxious, raced around to the passenger's side, scooped him up, then locked the van and went through the gate, making sure to close it behind me. The building was an old Victorian property, red brick-fronted with a large, ugly glass and metal addition. The porch had seemingly been stuck on to the front with little thought as to design, but it was a quiet interlude before the clinic proper, so I took a breath then pushed open the inner door and entered a world very familiar but always a surprise.

Some veterinary clinics are modern places, many are converted houses or old shops changed to accommodate the reception area, waiting room, and consultation rooms. This was definitely one of the latter. The interior had been re-configured, with the ground floor divided into a large, open-plan space with doors off to one side. The main area was filled with rows of chairs and bench seats with a long reception area at the far end.

All eyes turned to us as the door hissed closed. Dogs barked, cats meowed and spat from carriers, the owners either fretting, resigned, or smiling, depending on the severity of the issue and how their pet was coping.

Above all else, was the unmistakable smell of bleach combined with the fear of the animals and the nasty tang of one too many accidents having been hurriedly cleaned up from the black and white chequered tile floor. The handful of people present kept their animals close for fear of them having a nervous bowel movement, one eye on their dog, the other on the door in case they needed to make a run for the grass with poo bags clutched tightly.

My main focus was on Anxious, though, and I paid the room scant attention as I hurried to the reception counter, trying to avoid the racks of expensive, specialist pet food, the flea medication, and the lure of brightly coloured toys with squeaks inside designed to make all owners grind their teeth and wonder what on earth they'd been thinking.

Two receptionists were busy typing as I approached. One was a young woman with a stylish short crop of bleached-blond hair, her ears festooned with hoops, bars, and chains in a strange interconnected array, and sporting bright red lipstick. The other woman was in her sixties, and very slender, with brown hair, although grey roots were beginning to show. Both had pleasant smiles when they looked up from their monitors.

"Hi. Max Effort," I panted.

"What is?" shouted the elder lady, causing me to step back, the clientele to gasp, and the dogs and cats to whine.

Anxious trembled in my arms as he held up his paw.

"Aw, will you look at the little guy?" gushed the younger woman, her face a mask of sympathy and concern.

"What's a max effort?" the elderly woman shouted again, causing the other to wince and sidestep around the counter.

"It's my name. I called to see if you could fit Anxious in. He hurt his paw."

"He doesn't look anxious. He looks worried," belted Mrs. Shoutsalot.

"That's his name. His name is Anxious, mine is Max Effort."

"Do you hate your parents?" giggled the receptionist who I noted was named Beatrix Erin Collins by her name tag.

"Beatrix, I do, and I shall continue to do so. They still don't get that it's nuts to call their son Max when they know their own surname."

"Call me Erin. Everyone does." Erin smiled warmly as she rubbed Anxious' head.

"And you call me Max. Anxious hurt his foot on a tin can and I'm worried it might get infected. He's been very heroic, but I think he might need stitches."

"The vet won't be long, then we'll rush him right in."

Anxious whimpered and tried to hide in my arms as he shook.

"He doesn't like that word," I confided. "Can you say doctor instead?" I asked with a wink.

"Of course," giggled Erin. "We get that a lot. Let's take your details and I'll send a message to the 'doctor' who will fix Anxious right up."

While Erin took my details and fired off a message to the vet, the other lady, Agatha Plum, dealt with the waiting customers by screaming out names then muttering as she clattered on her old keyboard, trying her best to put it out of its misery.

Confused by the noise, Anxious burrowed into me and I stroked his back to soothe him. The paperwork was dealt with soon enough, so we took a seat but were called in almost immediately by Agatha. I took Anxious over to the door she pointed to as it opened and a man roughly my age smiled at us.

"Hi, I'm Dr. Parker, and I'm guessing this is Anxious?"

"Hi, yes." I explained what had happened as we entered the small consultation room. A metal table took up most of the space, with a desk in the corner and shelves of equipment. As with all such rooms, it was simple, minimally furnished, and easy to wipe down.

"Now, let's take a look at you, Anxious," said Dr. Parker.

"Be brave for Dr. Parker, Anxious. He's going to make it all better," I promised.

"Please, call me Ollie. And yes, Anxious, we'll have you fixed up in no time."

Anxious looked from me to the vet warily, then lifted his paw for Ollie to examine it. He whined sadly but let Ollie do his job, and a moment later the kind vet released Anxious, nodded, then made several notes on his computer.

"We'll take him through to the back and sedate him so we can shave around the cut, clean it out, and give him a few stitches. It's nothing to worry about, and we'll do it right now just so you can take him home in a few hours."

"Really? That's great! Wow, I wasn't expecting such fast work."

"We look after our furry friends. It's what we're here for," he beamed.

We both glanced at the door as the noise levels rose. Dogs barked, and people shouted, but Ollie just sighed then turned to me, smiling, as he shook his head. "Sometimes this place is a madhouse. Some dogs get very stressed, and very vocal."

"It's understandable. It's a strange environment for them, with so many new smells."

"Absolutely. But Anxious has done amazingly. I'll... Gosh, what on earth is happening out there?"

"Someone really doesn't want to see the doctor," I laughed as a woman shouted and then an incredibly loud bang sent me hurriedly grabbing Anxious and ducking for cover.

Ollie crawled under the table and I joined him with Anxious cradled tightly in my arms.

"What was that?" I gasped. "You ever heard that before?"

"It sounded like a gunshot. But it couldn't be, could it?"

"We better take a look. Maybe something got broken."

"It was very loud."

"I know," I said, worried. Nevertheless, I crawled out from under the table, held Anxious tight, and eased open the door.

A wall of sound hit as another explosion rocked the building and smoke billowed. Coughing, I raced into the waiting room and stumbled to the door to let fresh air in, only to find it was already open. A white van peeled away from the car park, tyres squealing, as I turned and noted Ollie at the door to the consultation room before he was shrouded in a cloud of smoke.

"Is everyone alright?" I shouted above the din of a dog howling and people coughing and moaning in confusion.

"Where's my Pipkin?" wailed a woman. "I can't see her anywhere."

"Was there a bomb?" a man asked.

"Where's my dog? Here, boy," another man wailed.

"Help! Somebody help," screeched a distraught lady.

"Aggie, Aggie, what's wrong?" screamed Erin from what sounded like the reception area.

Still clutching Anxious, I fought through smoke that was already beginning to clear, and stopped when Ollie grabbed me.

"Was there a shooting?"

"I don't know. But I think your receptionist is hurt."

"Be careful," warned Ollie as we headed towards the faint shape of the reception counter.

Smoke grew denser as we moved cautiously, sticking close to the wall. What I didn't understand was why it didn't smell like a fire, more like...

"It's just a smoke bomb like you get from machines at nightclubs," I spluttered, my throat dry and my eyes watering, but at least there were no noxious fumes.

"Help me, please," pleaded Erin.

"Hey, what's that?" called a man, then it sounded like he thudded to the ground.

"What is happening here?" demanded Ollie, exasperated by the lack of vision.

"I have no idea."

"It's all wet," the man called. "It's thick. It's... I think it's blood."

"Aggie's choking," shouted Erin.

With my heart racing, Anxious whining, the room a raucous riot of shouts, screams, and calls for pets, several other doors opened from the back, the smoke cleared as windows were opened, and the true extent of the madness was revealed.

A male nurse in green scrubs lay prone on the ground, blood pooled around him from the chest wound. The man who had been shouting sat beside him, staring at his bloodied hands, numb with shock. People screamed as they realised what had happened.

Erin called again, so I raced over with Ollie and found her behind the reception counter, her eyes unfocused, struggling to get Agatha sitting upright.

"It's stuck! Help me," she pleaded, tugging at a rubber toy jammed into Agatha's mouth, the woman bright red and clawing at her throat.

I dropped down and released Anxious then crawled over and said, "Try to relax. Don't fight it. Stay calm and I'll pull it out, okay?"

Wild-eyed, Agatha moved her hands from her neck and I took hold of the hard rubber toy and with a firm grip on her jaw I gently prized it free.

Agatha coughed and gasped, her eyes streaming, a nasty lump on her forehead.

Erin leaned back against the wall and I noted a similar bump on her head, the skin split. A trickle of blood trailed to her eye and she rubbed at it, then frowned as if she hadn't even realised she was hurt.

"Are you both okay? What happened?"

"I... we... It went smoky, then we must have been hit with something," wheezed Erin.

"I was hit," shouted Agatha, "then someone stuffed that toy into my mouth and everyone started screaming."

"He's dead," yelled Ollie. "Riley's dead!"

I stood, said, "Wait here," to the two women, then turned back to Ollie. He was crouched beside Riley, the man who'd discovered him still sitting there, trembling, and very green.

"Is he definitely dead?" I asked.

"Yes, I just checked. Someone stabbed him. What happened?" he asked the man beside us.

"I... don't... know. The room filled with smoke, the dogs began to bark, then there were these loud noises. I... I think someone was swinging a baseball bat, but then I couldn't find my dog and I just don't know."

A nurse, Ollie, and the receptionists gathered around as the few customers and I stood and surveyed the carnage.

"Um, where are the animals?" I asked.

Soon enough, it became very clear that the only animal still present was Anxious, who limped from behind the counter and whined at my legs. I held him tight as the sirens of the emergency services grew louder.

Chapter 2

With the waiting room in utter carnage, the displays knocked over, blood on the floor, several piles and puddles from stressed animals, at least I hoped it was, but no actual animals, everyone made a beeline for outside, leaving the poor dead man, Riley, alone.

The *whoop whoop* of an ambulance closed in, intermittently drowned out by police sirens, as we gathered in the bright, cheery gardens, the sunlight dazzling.

A German Shepherd barked loudly and a delighted owner raced over to retrieve him, but he was the only person who could find their pet. I counted just five other stunned owners, and from the overheard conversations it seemed we were missing two dogs, a cat, one parrot, and a tortoise. That made six customers, the vet, two receptionists, a female nurse, plus me and Anxious.

Several people nursed head wounds, and others had been hit on their bodies, with only one person avoiding any injury. Nobody understood what had happened, how, or why, but it was clear this was a planned attack and they'd been after the animals.

"How are you doing, Anxious?" I asked, holding him tight for fear he might be stolen.

He licked my face eagerly, relieved to be out of the clinic, most likely believing it was over. He still needed his stitches, but I guessed that would have to wait now.

"Thank you for saving me!" bellowed Agatha Plum as she stood so close I could smell her breath and noted that one of her eyes was green, the other blue.

"Yes, thank you," gushed Erin, brushing at her chopped hair, smearing blood over the raggedy blond fringe.

"You're welcome. It was the least I could do." I rubbed at my own hair, the long length still a surprise as it had been short for so many years as I battled my way through kitchens, striving for perfection, never satisfied. My beard rasped as I smoothed it down, sure I looked rather wild, feeling anything but the hippy at heart I'd slowly been letting myself become as my vanlife adventure continued.

"You have nice eyes," said Erin, then reddened as she smiled.

"Thanks. And so do you. Very pale blue. And yours are unusual, Agatha."

"All the women in my family have mismatched eyes," Agatha roared, causing me and Erin to step back and Anxious to paw at my arm. "Who did this? Why would anyone kill poor Riley? He was a nice boy and a fine nurse."

"It's barbaric," said Ollie as he joined us, rubbing his cheeks vigorously, his clean-shaven jaw reddening under the pressure. He ran trembling hands through his stiff, short brown hair, tugging at it like he was more concerned about his appearance than anything. It was the stress, that was clear, and he looked ready to collapse.

"I think you need to take a seat," I suggested. "You don't look so good."

"I don't feel it. I thought there was a gunman and everyone would be dead, and that the clinic was on fire. Imagine if that happened. The animals would be killed. We have a lot here as we have kennels and those in recovery. What are we going to do? Who stole our customers' pets?"

"I have no idea, but we'll find out. Let the police do their job, tell them anything you can, and then we'll talk later, okay?"

"Sure. Yes, thank you. Max, you seem like you know what we're supposed to do. Why is that?"

All three watched me carefully as I considered what to say for a moment, then decided the truth was the best course of action. Once I'd explained about how I kept coming across murders and mysteries, and helped to solve them, and shyly admitted that my new vanlife seemed to be tied to me having found my true calling of helping out the various local communities I visited, they said they'd heard about some of the cases, and hoped I'd stick around.

"I haven't got any choice," I admitted. "Anxious still needs his stitches, and my van's not fit to drive. It kept juddering and smoking as I drove here, so I need a mechanic to come out or get it towed."

"My brother can sort it out for you," said Erin. "He loves VWs, has a campervan of his own, and runs a garage. I'll give him a call."

"That would be great! Thank you."

With shaking hands, Erin phoned her brother, explained what had happened, then asked if he could come to look at my van. I was surprised she'd made the call after so much stress, but I think she was happy to have the distraction.

As she hung up, the first of the emergency services arrived, and soon we were swamped with all manner of official personnel, including the fire brigade, the police, paramedics, detectives, and a lot of smartly dressed people clearly high up in the police department.

Luckily, I didn't recognise any of them, being far enough away from my last murder case for it to be a different branch dealing with things here. Nevertheless, it seemed that my reputation preceded me, and once I'd given my name and recounted every detail I could recall, I was told in no uncertain terms that in Harlech they did things differently and I would absolutely be locked up for interfering if I didn't stay away. But then the detectives in charge laughed, said they were only joking, and if I could solve the case then good luck to me. They wandered off still laughing about it, leaving me feeling rather put out but more determined than ever to discover who had killed the nurse and stolen the animals.

The press of people was stressing me and Anxious out, so I retreated to the campervan and entered my home on wheels with a deep sigh of relief. The retro interior, complete with striped fabrics, compact kitchen, and now very familiar small sink and hob calmed my nerves as I settled on the bench seat with Anxious curled up beside me.

Now about as well-organised as I could make it, I knew the interior intimately and had grown to love this cramped space that conversely allowed me so much freedom. Feeling rather smug, I put the kettle on, then figured I should do a good deed so filled it to the brim, whacked up the gas, and gathered as many mugs as I could and a stack of plastic cups for emergencies. With a box of teabags, milk, and sugar, I busied myself setting up my table outside the campervan, and even opened a few packs of biscuits. The good ones!

Having something to do calmed my frayed nerves, and despite what had happened, I couldn't help smiling at the rising tide of anticipation I felt about uncovering the truth behind this latest grisly murder. Was that bad? I shouldn't be excited, I should be sad for the poor man who died and everyone who had been battered and their animals stolen. But yet again, I felt that this was my calling. These things kept happening because I was good at uncovering exactly who was responsible.

There was no doubt I had a fine eye for detail, picked up on things not even the police noticed, and was able to fit the pieces of these strange puzzles together until the culprit was uncovered. I would do it again, or at least try.

The kettle whistled so I turned off the gas, left a very stressed Anxious sleeping on the bench seat, and took everything I needed outside.

The police were all over the scene, still talking to people, taking details, descriptions of animals, and more had arrived while I was inside. People from the coroner's office, photographers, crime scene investigators, the list went on.

I focused on those who had been present through all this, though, watching how they acted, what they did, yet nothing jumped out as unusual given the circumstances.

"Erin, do you want a cup of tea?" I asked as she wandered around looking like a lost soul.

"Tea? Oh, yeah, wow, that would be perfect! I'm parched."

"Is there enough for me?" asked Ollie, sweating under the heat of the day and the stress he was undoubtedly under. "We can't go inside to use anything, but we need to go and check on the animals soon."

"Sure, there's plenty. What about you, Agatha?"

"Yes please," she barked, smiling wanly as she took Erin's arm and the three approached.

I made us drinks then put the kettle back on and joined them as we watched events unfold.

"Any idea why anyone would steal animals?" I asked.

"I bet they want to sell them," said Agatha, her tone as loud as ever, but I was getting used to it now and kept my distance to save my eardrums.

"Is this a problem in the area?"

"It's happened now and then over the years," sighed Ollie, cupping his mug and taking a sip. "I've been here for five years after moving from Liverpool to take over the practice, and we've had a few cases of dogs being stolen. Nothing for a long while though."

"And I've worked here for thirty years," said Agatha, "and I've never known anyone do anything violent. My head really hurts."

"You should probably go to the hospital," I said, wondering why she hadn't, Erin too.

"The paramedics looked us over and said we were fine. Just a nasty gash, but no stitches needed, and no sign of anything to worry about," said Erin.

"That's good. So, Ollie, is this your practice?"

"I bought it to have my own business, and I love it here. Near the coast, lots of great walks, ideal for starting a family. I have two little ones now, and my wife adores the area. She's from around here."

"That's great. What about you, Erin?"

"Born and bred in Harlech," she said proudly. "This is my first job, and I don't ever want to leave. I enjoy working for Ollie, and Aggie's a hoot."

I looked to Agatha then back to Erin for any sign of her joking, but she was serious. They clearly got on very well.

"Both of you do a stellar job," said Ollie, beaming with pride. "You saved the business. I could never do it without you. We have, or had, two nurses, and there was another qualified vet but..."

"Yes, what?" I asked as he trailed off and his attention drifted to the entrance.

"It's a sore point," said Erin, smiling in sympathy at Ollie. "It's okay. We'll find someone else."

"If we don't get run out of business first. But thanks for sticking with me."

"We'll never leave. We love it here," said Erin.

"That's right," said Agatha. "We want to work for someone who cares, not a faceless corporation."

"What's this about? Could it be relevant?" I asked.

My new friends exchanged concerned glances and something seemed to click.

"He wouldn't, would he?" whispered Erin.

"He'd sell his granny for a pair of driving gloves. I bet he killed Riley and took the pets," hollered Agatha.

"Don't be ridiculous. He might be a snake, but he'd never go that far."

"Are we talking about another vet?" I asked.

"That traitor Patrick might be involved," said Agatha through pursed, thin lips like she was sucking on a sour sweet.

"No, he's a good guy really, just looking out for himself and his future," chided Ollie. "Max, it's who he works for that's the problem. A new veterinary clinic opened a few years ago, a corporate type business with practices throughout the country. Nothing wrong with that, and they replaced an old clinic that was up for sale. But they poached my staff, took the other vet, and it's not easy to find a replacement. It's not the fact it's a big business, it's the fact that the manager is not a great guy."

"Not a great guy?" blurted Erin. "He's an utter snake and a pariah. He poached Patrick, that's the other vet, tried to get us to leave, too, and when we wouldn't he got super weird about the whole thing and said he'd make sure we lost our business and he'd get us shut down. He hates the competition and thinks he's better than us."

"That sounds harsh."

"It was," sighed Ollie. "But the important thing is that we're still up and running. We're a proper team."

"A true family," said Agatha.

"Agatha, you like it here then? You're staying?" I asked.

"Love, call me Aggie, and yes, of course. As I said, I've been here for decades. Seen many changes, but Ollie's the best boss I've ever had."

"I don't even feel like a boss," said Ollie. "I just wanted a proper future for my family so figured I should stop working for others and run my own practice. It's the best decision I ever made, but I could do without creeps trying to spoil it."

"Would this guy stoop to murder?" I asked. The question sounded ridiculous, but after recent experiences I knew what seemingly regular people were capable of.

All three laughed nervously, then Ollie said, "Leo might be a despicable man, but he's no killer. One thing I do know, he loves animals the same as we do. He just hates people."

"I'm so sorry about your friend. Riley, was it?" I said as we turned to watch the paramedics take him away on a stretcher.

"He was a gifted nurse and cared about this place deeply. He helped with so much, like we all do. He'll be sorely missed."

"He really will," agreed Erin.

"We need justice," hissed Aggie, her face tight with a frown. "What possible reason could anyone have for killing poor Riley? And where are the innocent animals? What if they're going to eat them?" Her trembling hand shot to her mouth as she gasped, eyes wide as she scanned the area.

"Nobody's going to be eating tortoises or parrots," soothed Ollie. "Especially when they most likely know how much they cost."

"And how much is that?" I asked.

"An absolute fortune. The parrot is worth a few thousand, and the tortoise maybe five hundred. The dogs more, the cat less."

"Nobody wants cats," said Erin.

"I love cats. You know that!" scolded Aggie as she shook her head. "I have three," she said with pride. "They're my babies."

"We love the animals in our care," said Erin, "but you can't beat dogs."

Several of the owners grieving for their pets began to converge, nobody knowing what to do or where to go once they'd finished being interviewed, so I asked if anyone wanted a cuppa then raced to turn off the kettle as it whistled angrily.

Everyone was grateful for something to do and a cup of tea to calm their nerves, so before long the sad owners had assembled and several officers were following their noses and coming to investigate. With a sigh, I put the kettle back on after pouring drinks, until soon I had a real crowd around the van. People speculated as to what the motive really was, talking animatedly about the smoke bomb that had been used, the bruises they'd received, but mostly lamenting the loss of their pets.

Several people had heard of me, and began asking questions once word got around I'd been the one who solved the recent poisoned pickle problem, and a few had even heard about the issue at the seaside and the problems in Rhyl. Despite not chasing any kind of infamy, I was now known, and I vowed that after this latest stop on my trip around the country I'd head further south into England and keep a low profile.

But first I had to get Anxious treated, Vee fixed, and look into this terrible case.

"What are you looking so wistful about?" asked Erin.

"Just thinking about Anxious and the van and whether I should get involved in this."

"Max, you have to," snapped Erin. "You said it yourself. It's your calling. You helped solve those other crimes, and this is why you began the new life. It's what you're here for. It can't be coincidence that you arrived exactly when such a terrible thing happened. You have to help."

"But the police will be all over this. I don't want to get in their way."

"Come on," said Ollie, "please? Of course the police will investigate, but an extra pair of eyes and ears can't hurt. Max, this is fate. We need your help. I need your help. Look, don't say anything yet. Just hang around and give it a day or two before you decide. It might be finished with by then. You need to let Anxious get better, and you need to recover too. It's a huge shock for everyone, so let's not be hasty about anything. I'm going to ask the cops if we can go back inside. We need to check the animals, and I need to fix Anxious." With a nod, Ollie walked like a zombie over to the detectives.

"He's taking this really hard," declared Aggie. People backed away until, like the eye of the storm, a large area of free space expanded around her. They were clearly locals and used to her unbelievably loud voice.

"He's done so well building up the business, even after losing Patrick to the other practice. Ollie's worked extra hours to keep things going, but we're just a small clinic and it's hard on him."

"Okay, I'll stick around," I laughed, then turned serious as those who'd lost their animals muttered. "No offence intended. Sorry about that."

Ollie returned and said he was allowed to go inside and could look after Anxious now, so I woke the little guy up and followed the three of them and a woman I hadn't met before, the other nurse, around the side of the clinic, past a series of very nice kennels, and into the building at the rear.

Anxious was, well, he was anxious, so I soothed the scared guy and reassured him that he'd be fine, then waited while the others checked on the animals then returned.

"Now, let's get you fixed up, shall we?" said Ollie softly as he stroked Anxious' back.

My best friend in the whole world whined, eyes pleading with me to save him from whatever the vet was about to do, but I reluctantly handed him over then remained by his side while they sedated him and began to clean up the wound.

Ten minutes later it was over, and Anxious was sitting in a nice warm bed. He was groggy, but coming around from the anaesthetic, and seemingly already on the mend. His tail wagged as the nurse, a woman called Pip, sat beside him and spoke softly. I joined her and told him how brave he'd been and that it was over now. Anxious looked at the door with true longing while Pip and I stifled a laugh as he cocked his head.

"Give it a few more minutes, Anxious," said Pip, mock-serious. "You can go outside soon, I promise."

"Thanks for looking out for him."

"It's why we're here. It's what we do. Hey, I heard all about you. Are you staying?"

"For a while, yes."

"That's great. Catch these buggers, Max. For all our sakes."

"I'll try my best."

Chapter 3

The staff went about their business of checking on the few other patients, exercising the dogs housed in the kennels, and dealing with the police as necessary. Even at the back of the building the inquiry was loud, voices raised as various teams called to each other or requested assistance. But as time wore on so it quietened down, and so did the stressed animals.

Anxious had a nap, drowsy after the anaesthetic, so I simply sat on the floor beside him and let things play out. For a change, it felt good to be away from the chaos that ensued when someone was killed, rather than me remaining in the thick of things. There were too many people, too much going on, and I needed peace, time alone after dealing with everything. I enjoyed the company of others, but not too many, and not for too long. People were alright, but so was being alone. And when was I ever truly alone anyway? Never, because I had my best friend in the whole world right beside me. Speaking of best friends...

"Oh no!" I groaned, putting my head in my hands. "I haven't told Min."

After the pub poisonings, I'd kept a low profile with my incredible ex-wife. She had her job, I had my travels, and after seeing so much of each other I'd just called a few times as I didn't want to come across as pushy, or ruin what we seemed to have going on. She wanted at least a year to find out what it was like to truly be herself with no husband to worry about or ex-husband to deal with. Our first year of being divorced had now come and gone, but that'd mostly been coping with the aftermath and everything settling down.

We both realised we still loved each other very much, not that I had ever stopped loving her, but time was needed to let things work out how I knew, or at least hoped, they would. Which was to be together again.

We both felt it, but Min needed her independence, never mind that she'd come to check on me the day after I started my new vanlife!

Should I call? She had work, and her own life to lead, but I knew she'd be cross if I kept her in the dark. Min loved Anxious as much as I did, and would want to know about his accident. And who was I kidding? She'd want to know about someone being killed whilst I was at the vets. Of course she would.

Realising I was definitely over-thinking things, I left Anxious dozing and stepped outside into the heat. My stomach rumbled as I'd had no breakfast and it was well past lunchtime now, so that would be next on the agenda.

I called Min and explained what had happened; she was understandably upset about Anxious and concerned about me. When she said she'd come, I told her there was no need as she'd taken enough time off work recently and we were both fine. Much as I'd have loved her to visit, I didn't want to be a nuisance. In the end, she acquiesced and admitted that she did have several clients to see and it would be difficult to get away, so I promised to keep her updated, and to be careful. Min understood that I had a calling now. There was no longer any denying that these bizarre incidents were following me around the country, or I was following them. Either way, she knew I'd look into things and try to help out the veterinary practice and stop anything else bad happening.

"You okay, Max?" asked Erin as I hung up. "I just spoke to the detectives and they're finishing up soon. They've shut us down for obvious reasons, but we can do emergencies and will be allowed back inside the practice soon."

"That's great news. Not that you're closed, but that they're almost finished. And yes, I'm good. Any news? What did they say?"

"It was definitely a smoke bomb. Like tear gas but without the risk to people's health."

"Whoever did this didn't care about people's health. They stabbed the nurse."

"I know, right? It makes no sense. I told the detectives that. They made a good point, though, which was that it's much easier to get your hands on a smoke bomb than genuine tear gas. That's strictly off-limits to regular folk. Actually, it was a few smoke grenades. That's what they called them. I never knew, but you can buy them almost anywhere. People use them at parties, weddings, playing paintball, all kinds of things."

"Makes sense. Anything else?"

"Not really," Erin shrugged. "Riley was killed with a knife, but the killer took it with them. People were hit with a baseball bat most likely, and that was probably more to cause confusion than anything else."

"How did they see when nobody else could? I don't understand that. When I opened the door, the room was thick with smoke, so how could they find anything, let alone swing a bat at people, murder Riley, and take the animals too?"

"Infrared goggles," said Erin with a smirk.

"Of course! I hadn't thought of that. It wouldn't be like seeing normally, but enough to see heat signatures. That's rather wild, though, isn't it?"

"It's nuts, Max. Who does that? Someone, or maybe a few people, and I think it was more than one, came with smoke grenades, night vision goggles, baseball bats, and for what? Steal a parrot, two dogs, a tortoise, and a cat? It's crazy."

"Maybe that's exactly what they want everyone to think," I mused.

"How'd you mean?"

"I mean, maybe this has nothing to do with the animals and was just about killing Riley. A distraction."

"But why? He was a nice guy, just a nurse, not someone who deserved to be killed."

"I honestly don't know. The other motive might be as you said earlier. The other veterinary practice. A way to put Ollie out of business. Give him a bad reputation."

"That's what I said to the detectives when they asked who had a motive. They'll look into it, but they agreed with me that it's rather far-fetched. Ollie is closed while they investigate, but most likely he can open up again tomorrow. People might be rather put off for a while, but they'll understand, and certainly won't expect it to happen again."

"True. What about you? Are you okay? This is a lot to handle. You and Aggie both got hit on the head. Are you feeling alright?"

Erin prodded her lump tentatively and winced, but grinned and said, "I'm tough, and so is Aggie. We can look after ourselves. I'm twenty-six and can hold my own. You have to in a job like this."

"Working on reception?" I asked, nonplussed.

"Yeah, it's a war zone in there sometimes," she laughed. "Dogs going wild, people crying, or angry about the cost of operations. Believe me, it can get gnarly."

"I bet!" I chuckled.

"And don't even get me started on the cats. They're the worst of all. Have you ever tried to put a cat back in a carrier? They really don't like it."

"Can't say I have, but I can picture it. Erin, what's the deal with Aggie?"

"In what way?"

"She's, er, very loud. Does she need a hearing aid or something?"

"Nah, that's just Aggie. She hears fine, but for some reason she's always been loud. Super loud. It's how she is. Apparently, even when she was little, shouting was her default setting. She was born turned up to eleven. That woman never stops talking. She's hard-wired to keep her mouth open."

"I just wondered. I've never spoken to anyone who shouts so much."

"You get used to it. I don't even notice anymore. Probably because I'm deaf in my left ear now as that's the side she's on in reception," Erin teased.

"So what now?"

"My brother should be here soon, so hopefully you'll get your van fixed. I spoke to Pip, and she said Anxious should be okay to leave now if you want to take him."

"That's great! And I need to pay for this."

"No way! Max, you've been a great help, and Ollie said I absolutely was not to take any payment."

"If you're sure?"

"Absolutely. I have a few things to do, but I'll see you later. Max, you will help with this, won't you? I checked up on you," she said shyly, "and you've done some awesome stuff."

"Have you been snooping?" I teased.

"It's in my nature. A lot's happened to you lately."

"It sure has. I've only been at this vanlife a short while, but I keep finding myself up to my neck in intrigue."

"Then please stay and help us out. Our friend is dead, animals are missing, owners are distraught, and I know the police will work hard, but having you here will help too. Please?"

"Of course I will. I need to find a campsite though. I haven't booked anything and was going to check once I got to Harlech, but haven't had the chance."

"I know just the place."

Once I got the details from Erin, I returned to collect Anxious. He was fast asleep, but as I smiled at Ollie and Pip —who both looked exhausted and stressed—he opened his eyes and yawned.

"Hey there, sleepy. How are you doing?"

Anxious' tail thumped against the bed then he sat up, stood gingerly, put some weight on his poorly paw, and looked at me as if to check if he should.

"Take it easy, but I think you're alright. What do you think, Ollie?" We both turned to him.

"As long as he leaves the bandage alone he won't have to wear one of those funnels over his head, but, honestly, it was a minor wound. Just a clean-up and a few stitches. No real damage. He's fine. Walking shouldn't be a problem as the cut wasn't on the pad, but see how he goes."

"You hear that, Anxious? You're fine. Make sure you leave the bandage on."

Anxious barked happily, promising to do as Ollie said, then stretched out, yawned again, and trotted over to me, limping a little but keen to go.

"Thank you for this. Both of you."

"It was our pleasure. It's the least we could do," said Ollie.

"And Anxious is a real sweetheart," gushed Pip, grinning down at him as he rubbed against her leg. She bent and stroked his head, then stood and said, "I hear you're sticking around? Will you get justice for Riley and help find the animals? Customers are freaking out and we don't know what to tell them. What should we do, Max?"

"That's up to you. I don't know what you should do, sorry. What you usually do, I guess. Be kind, answer truthfully, and try to think who could do this."

"We will."

"I'll be here for a good few hours, I expect," I told them. "Hopefully, I can get the van fixed then I'll go to a campsite. But I'll stay in the area and look into this."

"Thank you so much," said Ollie.

With a nod, I left with Anxious in my arms.

Things were winding down outside, with most of the teams gone, but the entrance was cordoned off and I assumed would remain that way for the time being.

A truck arrived with the name of a garage printed on the side, so I assumed it was Erin's brother. Buoyed by the hope it offered, I went to greet a man about my age in oily mechanic's overalls as he jumped from the cab. He was thickset, slightly overweight, stocky like many Welshmen, with a crew cut, a blunt nose, but a friendly smile for me and an even bigger one for Anxious.

"Are you Max?" he asked, the Welsh accent stronger than his sister's but not as incomprehensible as many of the locals.

"That's me. Sorry, I don't think I got your name."

"I'm Rhys. And who's this?" Rhys ruffled Anxious' head and the recovering pooch wagged happily, his tail hanging free between my arms.

"This is Anxious. We came because he hurt his paw, but then everything went crazy."

"Yeah, Erin told me what went down. Crazy stuff, right?" Rhys rubbed a thick, oil-stained hand over his scalp then frowned. "Where is she? Is Erin okay? My sister acts brave, and is tough, but this was wild. Riley's really dead?"

"He is. It was very confusing, and the smoke made it impossible to see, but yes, he's gone. Erin is coping well, but it's been a shock for everyone."

"I'll go check on her, then you can show me what the trouble is. Yours, I presume," he asked, nodding to Vee.

"Yep, that's my home."

"Nice. I've always fancied vanlife myself."

"Erin said you own a VW?"

"Oh boy, do I! Actually, I have three," he mumbled, grinning. "Two are total rust buckets I picked up for next to nothing, the other is a 73 T2 that cost a bomb but still needs work. It's finding the time, and the money, but by the looks of it you sure had the money. Bet that cost a fortune."

"Quite a lot, but it's my home," I shrugged. "Now it's broken, and without being able to drive, I'm kinda stuck."

"Max, don't stress about it. I can fix anything, and VWs are my speciality. There's not that much to these air-cooled engines, to be honest. Especially the old ones. That a 67?"

"Yes, it is. Wow, you do know your stuff."

"I'm a total VW geek. I'll get you sorted, no worries. Don't tell me, it was juddering and the exhaust was smoking, right?"'

"How'd you know?" I asked, amazed.

"It's a common problem. See you in a bit?"

I nodded, then he went to find his sister. Anxious and I retreated to the campervan well away from the few remaining officers and teams. After settling him on the bench seat, I sorted out the cups from earlier then wiped everything down and washed up, feeling safe and secure inside Vee, no matter that I was currently stuck here.

Part of me was desperate to help the nice people I'd met, but the other half wanted to drive away now and forget the whole thing. Leave it to the professionals. I felt like an impostor, not someone who knew what they were doing. Because I didn't. People were relying on me, and it felt different because they were. The other times I'd got embroiled, it was more happenstance, not me purposely becoming involved because I was asked. Now there was more pressure and I wasn't sure I liked it one bit.

This life was meant to help me avoid such pressure. It was what I'd escaped by quitting my work. I reminded myself that nobody truly expected me to solve this as I was, after all, a burned-out ex-chef who was a hippy at heart and wanted a quiet, happy life, not a cynical ageing detective who lived for the job. No, I'd do what I could, help where needed, but there was no pressure because who was I to make any promises?

Feeling better, and also knowing there was nothing I could currently do, I pottered about in the camper, but when I went to wash my hands and the tap began to splutter, I realised I was almost out of water. With it being impossible to drive next to the tap and top-up from the outside, I went and filled my large container then opened the little flap over the funnel on the side panel that led directly to the water bottle underneath the sink. I then figured I should empty the grey waste, too, so disposed of it then cleaned everything down, pleased I was on top of things.

With my stomach rumbling, and no sign of Rhys yet, I made myself a simple sandwich with leftover ham from a one-pot wonder a few nights ago, then snuck outside before Anxious woke and pined for food. He had to wait a few hours or he'd get an upset stomach from the medications, but the little guy wouldn't understand that.

Leaning against Vee, I watched the last of the officers leave, the car park now virtually deserted after the commotion. The distraught pet owners had left, which was unfortunate as I hadn't had a chance to speak to any of them, something I would have to do, leaving just staff cars and the vans.

As I mulled things over, a black BMW with tinted windows pulled up silently, a new electric model that would have cost the earth. A smug looking man got out and closed the door proudly using the sleeve of his suit jacket, then admired the car for a moment before turning his attention to the clinic.

He grinned wickedly, then chuckled to himself before he began whistling, ambling forward with a cocky swagger. Closer to the front door, he tugged at the crime scene tape and actually laughed out loud before smoothing back his shiny black hair, adjusting his tie, and spitting.

Pip tore open the front door, face distorted with rage, her colour high, and hissed, "You disgusting man! How dare you! Laughing and spitting? I bet it was you, wasn't it?"

"Don't know what you're talking about," the man mumbled. Much of his bravado dissipating.

Pip lost the plot, and with a scream she launched at the man, fists balled, and they crashed onto the grass beside the path as she shouted and he tried to escape. But Pip was ferocious and straddled him, punching down on his chest, his shirt already torn.

I raced over, but Ollie came charging out, shouting for Pip to stop, and dragged her away, kicking and screaming, as the bewildered man sat there, face red, hair mussed, clothes ripped.

"She's utterly crazy! I'll have you for this, Pip, you just wait." A sly smile spread across his face as he added, "You'll be in real trouble now."

"Get lost, Leo," screamed Pip. "You smug git! Crawl back under the rock you came from. Go work for you big corporation and leave the real vets to their work."

"Ha, you're no vet, just a lowly nurse. I'm the real deal. I make a difference."

"Yeah, to your bank account. Not to people and animals. You slimy amoeba!"

"That's enough, Pip," warned Ollie, still holding her off the ground.

"He's a snake. Look at him. He was laughing, and he spat on the path."

"Did you spit?" asked Ollie, face darkening.

"She's off her rocker. I'm out of here." Leo stood, brushed himself down, frowned when he noted the tear to his shirt, then spun and marched back to his car.

He drove off with a squeal of tires and was gone.

Chapter 4

"Pip, what has got into you?" asked Ollie with concern as he released her and she stepped away.

"I... I'm sorry. I would never normally act like that."

"You could have really hurt him, or yourself," I said.

"Yes, I know, and that was utterly stupid. I just spied him through the door and couldn't stop myself. He was laughing at what happened, and then he spat. I just saw red. Riley is dead, people have lost their pets, and our business is affected, so I went wild."

"It's okay. Come on, let's get you back inside," said Ollie, turning to lead her away. He shrugged at me, shaking his head, but said nothing else.

"What was that about?" asked Rhys as he and Erin arrived.

Once I'd explained, they both tutted, but didn't seem unduly surprised.

"Pip has a real temper on her," whistled Rhys. "You have to watch yourself around that girl."

"Really? She was so nice earlier, and Ollie said it wasn't like her at all."

"Ollie protects his own," muttered Rhys.

"It's not like that," snapped Erin, shooting her brother a warning look.

"I say it how I see it. She's feisty."

"So am I. So are you. Pip's a sweetheart, and has been very good to me, but I admit she can be volatile sometimes."

"Violent with other people? I hate to ask, but you did want my help. I don't know any of you, so excuse me if I'm blunt, but has she been violent before?"

They exchanged another look, then Erin sighed and admitted, "Yes. The other vet who got poached from here, Patrick, used to be her boyfriend."

"Used to be?"

Erin fidgeted with her hair, then tugged at the tangle of silver at her ear as she kicked at the ground with her plain white trainers, but said nothing.

"Tell him," said Rhys. "Max is right. If you want this guy to help, he needs to have the full picture. Erin told me who you are, Max, and what's happened to you since you became a vanlifer. It sounds like you might be able to figure this thing out, so Erin is going to tell you, aren't you?"

"Yes, fine. Pip went spare when Patrick agreed to work for Leo. They had a massive fight right here in the car park, and she slapped him. They haven't spoken since. None of us have seen much of him, but we're friendly enough as we understand he's doing what he thinks is best for his future, but Pip won't even look at him, let alone speak with the guy she used to love."

"That's not so bad," I said, confused. "Not cool, sure, as hitting is never the answer, but she just slapped him?"

"It was no slap," said Rhys. "She broke his bloody nose. She punched him. I was here to pick up Erin and saw the whole thing. She right-hooked the poor guy, a right wallop it was, and then she launched at Patrick and had to be dragged off."

"The same as just now with Leo," I noted.

"Yeah, sounds like it. Anyway, enough of this. Pip might have a temper, but it just proves that she loves this place. She wouldn't be involved, and she was out the back anyway, wasn't she?" asked Rhys.

"I saw her come into the waiting room from the back, yes, just after the van drove off, so no, I don't think it was her. But it's best to have as much information about everyone involved as possible. What about this Leo? Could he have done it? I know you said no, Erin, but the way he acted was very nasty. Come to gloat, maybe? Check on his work?"

"He's too much of a coward," said Rhys. "Bloke's got no backbone. He's sneaky and devious, but no killer. Mate, you're barking up the wrong tree. But I wouldn't put it past him to hire a few thugs to do his dirty work. That's more his style. Come on, let's take a look at your camper." Rhys rubbed his hands together in anticipation. Erin rolled her eyes and left us to it.

"No way," Rhys gushed as I opened up the van and he peered inside.

"You like?" I grinned, taking absurd delight in another man approving of my taste in old campervans.

"Mate, it's bleedin' awesome! I'm dead jealous. It's got the original Westfalia kitchen, and all the rest of the fit-out. Even the little fold-down seat behind the passenger seat. Can I sit on it?" Rhys' eyes glazed over as I nodded, so he undid the catch and stepped up reverentially into the camper then perched on the tiny seat.

"I use it as a table sometimes, but I've been spending most of my time outside. I set up my outdoor kitchen and do most of my cooking that way."

"So sweet. Does the Rock-n-Roll bed work?"

"Yep, like a dream. Although it's a squeeze in here when it's down."

"I bet," he chortled, standing. "Hey, you have the pop-up roof too?"

"I do, but I don't think the extra bed that slides out is original. What do you think?"

He checked over the mechanism and grunted, then turned and said, "Not sure. But it's a damn fine job either way. Wow, even the original sink and everything."

"Most things are, apart from the electrics."

"You gotta move with the times," he said, nodding sagely. "Now, here's the big ask. Can I start her up so I can check what the issue is?"

"Of course."

Rhys treated the campervan with the utmost respect as he sat in the driver's seat then started Vee. I returned to the back and helped Anxious outside, who was desperate for a pee. He took his time sniffing around the enclosed garden, obviously the smells telling him so much about who had been here. He must have peed twenty times in different spots, trying to overpower the other dogs' scents, but he finished eventually.

Back at the van, Rhys was hard at work with all the doors open, tools by his side, fiddling with the engine at the rear of the vehicle. I still had to remind myself sometimes where it was, being so used to conventional cars.

"Any ideas?" I asked.

"Sure. It's simple enough. I'll be about half an hour."

"I'll pop the kettle on then. Perks of having your house with you."

"Sweet."

Anxious remained by Rhys, having decided that at least one of us needed to know rudimentary mechanics, so I left the guys to it and made a brew. Just as the kettle was boiling, Erin arrived, so I made her one too.

When I called for Rhys, he emerged from under the camper with a grin on his face and a smudge on his nose. "All fixed," he beamed.

"What? No way! That's great. Thank you, Rhys. What do I owe you?"

Rhys looked at his sister and didn't answer, so I turned and asked her, "Why are you shaking your head? Don't try to let him work for free. Everyone has to make a living."

"But you're helping us out. You shouldn't have to pay. Tell him, Rhys."

"That's right. If you're going to find whoever did this, that's brilliant for the town, so it's on me."

"No, I insist. I would have had to pay for a tow otherwise, and be stuck for hours or days without a place to live. Rhys, how much? And make sure it's the going rate."

Rhys nodded, and we shook, then I settled the bill, which was more than reasonable. With that out of the way, we drank our tea, chatting about this and that, until the topic of campsites came up.

"Is the one you told me about the best?" I asked Erin.

"Sure, they're all good. This one is lovely, although obviously not as nice as our place."

"Your place?"

"I meant our land. But you want fancy facilities, I suppose."

"I don't need facilities," I laughed. "A toilet, sure, but that's it. Why, what's your campsite like? And why not mention it?"

"It's not a campsite, it's more like a secluded patch in the garden. We're allowed a few tents or a campervan there, but that's it. There's a composting toilet, which isn't for everyone, but there's a hot shower, and unlike some places, we don't make you pay to get the hot water. That's always really sneaky."

"So I could stay at yours? Where is it?"

"Mate, it's the best spot in Harlech," gushed Rhys.

"You live there too?"

"We live together. It's the family home. Our folks are in Spain these days, so we never actually got to move out. Okay, I did for a while a few years back, but when things went sour with the missus I moved back home. Me and Erin live in the house, and we rent out the garden. It's a sweet spot."

"It's right in town, in Harlech, but up the hill a ways. You can see the dunes and the beach."

"And the castle, of course. Have you been?"

"Not yet, but it's on the itinerary."

"Oh, you have to go. It's beautiful."

"We'll be sure to check it out. So, can I stay at yours, or would that be weird?"

"Why would it be weird?" asked Erin.

"I'm not sure. Maybe because I'm looking into this, and you and Rhys are both suspects in a murder?"

Rhys spluttered his tea, then wiped his chin and asked, "You what, mate? I didn't do it and neither did Erin."

"I'm just messing with you!" I laughed. "But I suppose you are suspects to the police. What motive would you have? Maybe to sell the animals and the killing was an accident? Actually, maybe it was."

"But they still had a knife, and weren't afraid to use it," noted Erin. "Max, you trust us, don't you?"

"Yes, of course. Sorry, that was in bad taste. I know your friend died."

"We understand. Riley was a nice guy, and certainly didn't deserve to be killed."

"He was a good guy. I knew him quite well," said Rhys.

"Is there anyone who might have had it in for him? Anything he was involved in?"

"No way. He was as straight as they come. Too straight, actually. Took his work very seriously, studied hard to be a veterinary nurse, was training to become a qualified vet. Smart, studious, didn't hang out with any of the dodgy crowd."

"Who does?" I asked.

"Nobody." Rhys shrugged, but Erin elbowed him in the ribs. "Fine, but this is between us, okay?"

"Sure, Rhys, unless this is something the police should know about. I want to be straight with you guys, and that means I'm not going to withhold anything they should be told about. We good on that?"

"Sure, Max, we're good," grunted Rhys, then took a sip of tea.

"Well?"

"Aggie's old man is a bit of a tearaway."

"Aggie?"

"Yeah, he's trouble on bowed legs," agreed Erin.

"He served time," said Rhys, warming to the topic, "for armed robbery back in the day. Aggie's been working here for like forever, but her old man was never one to hold down a steady job. He's changed now, and does his best, but it's why she's always worked. Someone's gotta bring home the bacon, right?"

"I guess. So she stuck with him even though he's a crook?"

"He's a sweetheart, but had issues," said Erin. "He's different now, but years ago, and this is going way back to when Aggie first got the job here, he was a right nutter and ended up getting sent down for robbing a post office with a sawn-off shotgun."

"Wow, that's surprising. Aggie doesn't seem the type to have a gangster for a husband."

"Takes all sorts," said Rhys brightly. "But this is old news and water under the bridge. He served his time, Aggie got this job, and when he came out she stayed here and he did a bit of this and that. He's a handyman now, goes all over town doing whatever. He has contracts with a few places. He comes here, right, Erin?"

"Yes, whenever Ollie needs work doing. And he does stuff for other businesses too. Gets all over."

"Okay, thanks for telling me. But what do you guys think? Could he have been involved in this?"

"And risk hurting Aggie?" gasped Rhys.

"You don't know him at all," tutted Erin.

"No, I don't. So why are you so shocked by the question?"

"They absolutely dote on each other. Real lovebirds. You see them around town sometimes, holding hands, laughing and joking. They're well-known."

"And everyone always hears them coming. Aggie, at least. Her husband, Kent, is the opposite. Real quiet type. You have to lean in really close to hear him, and he has a strong accent. Mostly, they speak Welsh anyway, which is common, but we always speak English now."

"But you can speak Welsh?"

"Sure. We're in Wales," said Rhys, nonplussed.

"I know, but it's different up here to other parts of the country, especially South Wales. Down there nobody speaks Welsh, and it isn't even their first language."

"Now that's weird," laughed Erin.

"Hey, that's nice. Whose coat is that jacket?" asked Rhys, pointing to my waterproof coat hanging inside the camper for damp early morning dashes to the toilet block.

"Um, mine," I said, shrugging. "But don't you mean whose coat is that coat?"

"Do I?" wondered Rhys, frowning.

"You said, 'whose coat is that jacket?'" I prompted.

"Yeah, and? That's what you say, isn't it?" he asked Erin, nonplussed.

"Course you do. It's tidy, too."

I smiled, but wasn't making fun of them. Sometimes the Welsh idioms were hard to fathom, like 'tidy' meaning nice, but it was part of the beauty of the UK. Everywhere you went, local dialects and sayings were so entrenched that only an outsider thought anything of them.

"Very tidy," agreed Rhys. "That's why I asked." Rhys winked at Erin, who stifled a giggle. I was beginning to think it was me who was being laughed at, but I chuckled and took it in the spirit intended.

"Now, should we check on Vee?" I asked.

"Who's Vee?" asked Erin.

"My campervan. Not very original, but it's her name."

"Aw, that's sweet. And I like your number plate."

"Yeah, very cool, mate."

"Thanks." We moved to the front and I smiled as I looked at the private number plate I'd bought to surprise Min on the day I began my new life. MAX M1N. Silly, but it meant she was always here with me in spirit if not in hot body!

"Who's Min?" asked Rhys.

"Rhys! You shouldn't pry," warned Erin.

"It's fine. She's my ex-wife, and best friend besides Anxious. We split up a year ago after I'd been a terrible husband for a long time. I used to be a chef and was never around, and always pre-occupied and stressed. She finally had enough when I did something dumb."

"Max, you don't seem the type to act like that," said Erin with sympathy. "You're so laid back."

"I was an utter idiot. Blew the best thing in my life. But we're best friends now, and I'm trying to win her back. I packed in my job, sold a lot of stuff, gave her the house, and now I live a free life. It's only been a few weeks, mind you. But so far I'm loving it."

"A roving detective. What's the saying, home is where you park it?" said Rhys.

"I like that! Good one."

"So you really do still love her?" asked Erin.

"Very much. She still loves me, too, but it's hard for her after what happened. We hang out a lot as she's been coming to stay with me, and I've promised to give her a year to find herself and so I can prove I'm a changed man."

"Then well done to you," beamed Erin. "You admit your mistakes and are trying to be a better man. That's commendable."

"Yeah, nice one, mate." Rhys slapped me on the back then added, with a glint in his eye, "Now, let's go take Vee for a spin. Erin, you bring my van back with you. I'll get Max set up at home."

"Don't you have work?" I asked.

"Yes, mate, but it's my garage so I can nab an extra hour," he laughed.

"And I still have things to do here. We need to walk the dogs, arrange for some to be collected, and I want to be here for Ollie."

"When you have time, can you get me a list of the people who were here and their addresses?" I asked. "I'd like to go and visit them. Is that allowed?"

"I'll ask Ollie, but I don't see why not. Nobody will object if they know you're trying to find their pets. I'll see you both later." Erin turned to go, then paused and said, "But you do know it's bound to be that toad, Leo, don't you?"

"I thought he wasn't the violent type?"

"He isn't, but he's got money, and he's got motive, and there are plenty of people around here who would do anything for some quick cash."

"She's right, Max. It's bound to be Leo. The police will have already talked to him, is my guess, and he came here to rub everyone's noses in it and show that they had nothing on him. It was him. You can count on it. It might never be proved, but yeah, it's him."

"Then I'll be sure to check him out first."

I helped Anxious into the van, then let Rhys test-drive Vee. He was like a small child with a new toy, albeit a very large, extremely old one, as he pulled out of the car park carefully.

Once we got up to speed, I could feel the difference immediately.

"It's driving great!" I said happily. "I can tell it's better than ever."

"Yes, mate, it's what I do best. Feels awesome. Don't get all the upgrades the way some do, Max. Leave her be. This is how she's meant to run, and I wouldn't change a thing."

"I won't. Here, let me put on some sounds. Unless you think it isn't appropriate?"

"No, you go ahead. It's sad Riley's dead, but the living have to enjoy life. That's the whole point, after all."

I fished around and grabbed a tape, then put it in the ancient deck.

"A tape! Awesome!"

We drove into Harlech to the 80s and 90s mixtape I'd found when I cleared out my stuff. We belted out *Gold* by Spandau Ballet as we headed into town, grinning like dogs left alone in a butcher's shop.

Chapter 5

"This place is amazing!" I gushed, unable to stop smiling.

"Pretty cool, eh? The house isn't much, just a sixties bungalow, but the garden and views more than make up for it. You can see for miles, but it's protected from the worst of the wind too. It gets wild here in the winter when the gales howl through the hills, but we miss the brunt of it." Rhys was clearly proud of the family home, and rightly so.

Set on the side of the hill of Harlech town above the main street, and tucked behind rows of houses, the plot was unusually generous with gardens brimming with plants and a neat lawn—although it was a field really, it was so large—with mature silver birch casting beautiful dappled shade across the paths and borders.

At the bottom, where we now were, was a farm gate that gave vehicles access to the camping area. Little but an extension of the garden, but with a few more wild areas where nature had been left to do its thing. A section was mown short, so that was where Rhys parked, and now we were just ogling the view.

"You have a fire bowl there, and a stack of wood, but give me a shout if you want more."

"That's very generous of you."

"There's the compost toilet and shower," Rhys pointed to a weathered cabin tucked away discreetly behind a low holly hedge, "and there's running water. No electric hook-up, but I'm guessing your solar is working a treat at the moment anyway?"

"Yes, I haven't had to use any other power yet. Not that I've been running much. This place is magical, Rhys. You and Erin must love it here."

"Sometimes yes, sometimes no. Harlech's a strange place, Max. We get all these tourists, but as you saw, the main street has a few empty shops and we've gone through a lot of businesses over the years. It's the off-season that's the killer. The place is dead. Damn, I think I must have what happened on my mind. Let me rephrase. The off-season is very quiet. We're a very small town, just the main street and the hill leading down to the castle and then the main route along the coast. Not many jobs, not much to do beyond the beaches, so it gets very quiet."

"But you both stayed?"

"Yeah. It's home and we love it. It's where we belong. I have my business, Erin was lucky to get a job with Ollie and wouldn't dream of leaving, so here we are. Anyway, enjoy."

"Thanks. I'll see you around?"

"Sure. I'm here in the evenings, and I expect we'll bump into each other out and about. Take it easy. You've had a rough day, too, so relax. Enjoy the view, settle into things."

"That sounds like a fine idea."

Anxious pawed at Rhys' legs so got a nice head scratch for his trouble, then wandered off once satisfied he'd become the cutest dog in town.

Rhys waved, then headed towards the house, presumably before returning to work.

The ground was rather sloping even though Rhys had picked the perfect spot, so I decided to use the small ramps I'd spied others set up at the places I'd stayed recently. They were expensive, but a series of two small levelling ramps and a spirit level on the dashboard made an incredible difference to life inside the camper, and I wondered how I'd managed without them once I figured out the rather convoluted system for settling the camper on them correctly. It was at such times that Youtube seemed like a good invention, not a total time-suck that left you scratching your head two hours later and wondering how you ended up watching fifteen "shorts" when you'd been determined to only look at tutorials for guy rope knots and absolutely nothing else!

After rather too much to-ing and fro-ing, I stood back and admired the perfectly level campervan, and even popped my head inside to stare proudly at the centred bubble in the spirit level. And then I winced, because why on earth had I done this when I'd most likely be off out in a few hours? I'd walk instead. That would be a better idea. I wanted to explore the town anyway, and maybe we'd go to the beach later on or this evening.

But first, and most important of all, I needed to set up my kitchen.

I was an old hand at this now, so made short work of the sun shelter, tensioning the guy ropes like a pro, and the fold-out table was up in seconds, the latches secured so it wouldn't collapse—a costly and messy mistake I only made once. After unloading my stack of clear plastic containers with all my essentials, I laid out the portable stove, the other bits and pieces, a washing-up bowl, several tea towels and cloths, and felt as proud as any parent. It was familiar, comforting, and made me happy. A sense of place. That was important. I didn't want to feel like a stranger in my own life.

"Our home," I said, beaming at Anxious.

He barked in agreement, then curled up under the table and closed his eyes.

"I guess both of us like the comfort of home," I sniggered, then settled in my chair and admired the scenery.

Harlech had a magical feel to it, but I couldn't quite pinpoint why. The castle looked impressive, although it wasn't large by the standards of others on the north coast, but there was a smart visitor centre with a very good restaurant according to Rhys, so I'd check that out. Built in the 13th century, it offered incredible views out to the Irish Sea, with Snowdonia as a very impressive backdrop, and had become extremely popular with tourists ever since the new footbridge had been built and the visitor centre revamped.

The ice-cream from the tiny shop at the brow of the hill above the castle was apparently incredible, but I'd gone off the stuff ever since the slaughter at the seaside, so would skip that!

We'd taken the easier route into town, the road past the castle being too steep for Vee to cope with, and it truly was just the one short main street and two others leading down. That was it! So why did it feel so special? The air? The views? The people? I'd have to investigate and try to figure it out. But first I needed to rest.

Having decided to sit and mull things over, I was surprised to wake up and discover I'd been asleep for over an hour and it was now gone three.

"What a day, Anxious," I said, yawning, then almost choking as I snorted because Anxious had somehow managed to crawl into one of the plastic containers and was asleep on top of the tea towels. His head lolled over the side, tongue sticking out as he whimpered in his sleep. No doubt chasing rabbits in his dreams because he knew he couldn't currently do it in reality.

I stood and stretched as the little guy opened a lazy eye, frowned when he noted where he was, then hopped out, seemingly already on the mend as he padded over to the hedge without limping for a pee.

While he sniffed about, I gathered a few things before we set off down the hill into Harlech town. A few minutes later, we arrived in the heart of touristville. Compact gardens were bursting with hydrangeas, pelargoniums, and decorative hardy grasses, but many had to make do with the front step because everything was built so close together. Anxious whined at the door to a traditional sweet shop next to a charming cafe, the aromas from both businesses enticing, the jars of sweets brighter than the flowers in pots lined up against the wall like happy soldiers.

Across the road, a tourist shop sold postcards and anything you could possibly need for a day at the beach. I stopped to read a sign, surprised to find that the road down the hill to the right of the castle was the steepest road in the entire United Kingdom, and even the world! That couldn't be right, could it? Ffordd Pen Llech was famous and I hadn't even known it.

"How about that, Anxious?" I whistled. "Bet that would be a struggle to walk up."

Anxious stared from me to the sign to the road itself, then cocked his head and barked.

"I think we'll leave that for another day," I agreed.

Tourists milled about outside the shop or the ice-cream place, but I was rooted to the spot by a lone cyclist puffing his way up the hill, grimacing as he passed gawping tourists. He grunted as he gave it his all, then whooped as he made it to the level and stopped.

"Yes!" he shouted, beaming at me. "That was my third attempt today, but I did it. I cycled up the steepest road in the world."

"It's the second steepest, you nutty numpty" said a man happily, then licked his ice-cream. "They updated the record and now it's reverted back to a road in New Zealand."

"That's not right! They changed how they measure it. It's just a technicality," said a woman passing by. "I'm local, and I'm telling you now, we hold the record."

"I agree," said the cyclist. "They don't measure it properly over there. This is the steepest."

"Either way, good job," I told him, then Anxious and I hurried towards the castle before things turned nasty. They were still bickering as we turned the corner and found ourselves in a full car park outside the visitor centre.

An impressive wood and steel footbridge, gleaming in the sun, led from the modern building directly across a grassy moat to the castle entrance. People sat on the low wall surrounding the moat, eating and drinking, or snapping photos. It was a beautiful place, and we'd have to investigate properly, but for now I was happy to just sit on the wall and watch people coming and going.

Anxious nudged my leg with his nose, so I helped him onto the wall and he sat beside me, always a keen people-watcher, especially if those people might happen to have food and pause when they spied a delightfully friendly Jack Russell Terrier wagging his tail and showing off his poorly paw.

"You don't fool me," I warned, smiling. "No begging. Put your paw down."

The sneaky pooch lowered his leg, the bandage still nice and clean, but it had the desired effect and he soon made a few new friends and got several treats for his trouble.

Through the crowds, I spied Leo, the man who ran the other vets. He looked harried, and kept glancing behind him as though he thought he was being followed, and removed his suit jacket as he marched up the hill. With him being the number one suspect so far, I decided it wouldn't hurt to follow him. I helped Anxious down so he didn't put too much pressure on his leg, then we hurried after the spiteful vet as he turned the corner.

On the main road through town, I spun, unable to find him, then noted him glance back before ducking into an alley between the houses. We rushed over, followed him through, then stopped and watched as he slowed in a gravelled yard where several parked vehicles hugged the high walls surrounding the derelict land, making it very private.

Leo checked the area so we ducked out of the way, then I risked a peek. He was beside a white van, and stepped back when the door opened and a man in his sixties emerged. The stranger had rather bowed legs, wore dirty jeans, muddy boots, and a lumberjack shirt despite the heat. His silvering brown hair was thinning somewhat, long and tucked behind his ears. He was very tanned, had a thin, wiry frame, with a prominent aquiline nose and stubble, but you could tell he was strong and capable. It was Aggie's husband, Kent. I just knew it was. The bowed legs were the giveaway, plus the clothes of a handyman.

What were they doing? What were they talking about? Was this the van I'd seen earlier? Was it Kent who'd killed the nurse and stolen the animals? He wouldn't hurt his own wife, surely? Was he working for Leo? Doing his dirty work?

Leo was animated, gesticulating wildly, but their voices were low. With Leo's back to me, I couldn't see his face, but judging by the scowl on Kent's face the vet wasn't saying anything pleasant. Kent shook his head, then jabbed a finger into Leo's chest, who stepped back, brushed his arm away, and shouted, "Just sort it!" before turning and heading towards the alley.

I told Anxious we had to go, so turned and hurried into the bright day where tourists were chatting happily. We beat a hasty retreat to the sweet shop and I turned to the glass to watch Leo's reflection as he muttered to himself, brushing almost right past me before entering the cafe.

Follow Kent or Leo? I chose to keep an eye on Leo, so peered through the cafe window, watching covertly as he took a seat and placed an order. I sat at a table outside and ordered a coffee when the waitress arrived, keeping the chit-chat brief and general. Had everyone heard about the killing but was keeping quiet so they didn't scare away the tourists? My guess was yes, so I decided to do the same.

Leo must have been in a hurry, as not long after my drink arrived he left, so I took a few quick sips then followed him as he headed up the street.

Keeping a safe distance, it wasn't long before I discovered the other veterinary clinic. Set on a small industrial estate, it was a large facility with plenty of staff vehicles in the car park, but not very many customers' cars. Maybe they walked, or maybe people preferred Ollie's practice?

Leo entered through the front door, but there was no point following him inside, and little to be gained, so I was about to leave when I noticed a man watching him from the edge of the car park, a rake in his hand. What was there to rake at this time of year?

Intrigued, and always hopeful for the chance of some gossip, I sauntered over, sure to look relaxed and friendly.

"Hi," I said brightly.

"Hi. Little guy been in the wars, eh?" he asked, his accent so strong I had to make up half the words.

"Er, yes. Nothing too serious, although he had me worried for a while."

Anxious held up his paw, face sorrowful, clearly having a different opinion about the severity of his wound.

"How about a biscuit? Is that allowed?" the gardener asked, laying his rake down beside a collection of tools.

"Sure. You always carry them on you?"

"Doesn't everyone?" he chortled, handing a treat to Anxious who rubbed against his leg then settled between us to enjoy the unexpected snack.

"I know I do."

"I love dogs, and working here means I get to see plenty."

"I know this might come across as an odd question, and tell me to mind my own business, but did you hear about what happened at the other practice?"

"Of course! Terrible business. Poor Ollie."

"You know him?"

"I know everyone around here. Lived here my whole life." The gardener was a slim man with simple cargo shorts and a T-shirt revealing weathered arms and strong hands, his face dark from the sun, eyes shaded by a faded baseball cap. His hair was short and shockingly black. A true raven-haired man, which isn't as common as you'd imagine.

"Have you worked here long?"

"Long enough," he grunted, casting a scowl towards the door.

"It's like that, eh?"

"Yeah," he grumbled.

"So, again, tell me to mind my own business, but I don't suppose you know if Leo was out and about when it happened?"

"Who are you again?" he asked, dark eyes intense as he leaned forward and peered at me.

"I'm Max. I was there with my dog when it happened. Gas everywhere, people screaming, and the poor nurse was killed. The animals were taken too."

"So I heard. Sorry you had to witness that. I'm Dai."

We shook, then I asked again, "So, Leo? I only ask because it seems there's some rivalry and I'm trying to help figure this thing out."

"Ah, fancy yourself an amateur detective, eh?" asked Dai, grinning. "Good for you."

"Something like that."

"Then just between us, yes, Leo left about half an hour before I heard the attack took place. He returned an hour later looking all kinds of flustered, like he was just then, and he's been in and out all day. The police came and spoke to him earlier, but they weren't here long. I guess they think he's in the clear." Dai shrugged.

"Thanks for that. Does everyone know about the rivalry?"

"In a place like this?" Dai spluttered. "Max, everyone knows what colour underwear you're wearing," he sighed. "It gets annoying sometimes, but mostly it's nice. I work here because I need the money. You get me?"

"Sure."

"But Leo's a hard man to get along with, and backstabbing and politics ain't my thing. I just want to get the moss out of this grass and go on to my next job."

"Ah, that's why you have the rake. I was wondering. Thanks for the information."

"My pleasure. I'm not one to gossip, but if you think it might help. Don't go causing a fuss, Max. Folk around here don't appreciate strangers poking their noses in."

"It's the same everywhere, Dai, but if I can help, I will. I owe Ollie that much, and everyone else there. They've been very kind to me."

"They're a great bunch of people. I work up there, too, doing the gardens. Wish it was full-time, but what can you do? They're a tidy bunch."

"Very tidy," I agreed, suppressing a smirk at the use of the word for all things nice.

After a few more pleasantries, Anxious and I left and headed back into town. I carried him for fear of his leg hurting, but I think he was fine as he kept licking my chin. Taking advantage of the offerings in the local shops, I bought some nice bread, locally grown vegetables, and meat for the evening feast.

One-pot cooking was on the agenda like it was every night, and today I was especially looking forward to it. Groceries in my satchel, we made our way slowly back to the campervan where I left Anxious to rest while I set about preparing dinner.

Chapter 6

With a fire burning brightly in the fire pit, I began preparing dinner. Feeling adventurous, I was going to do a curry, but with a delightful twist. Rather than the usual frying pans, a pan for the meat, and a large pot to cook everything in, plus one for the rice, I was going to let the curry simmer for a few hours in my cast-iron pot over the fire then remove it and put the delicious dish into Tupperware to keep warm while I made the rice in the same pot. This would help clean up the Dutch Oven after the curry, and I would use the lid to warm through the cheeky naan breads I'd bought.

The heavy, expensive-but-worth-every-penny, pot was perfect for this, having a lid with a deep rim specifically designed to hold coals for a true oven-style bake, or flipped over and the flat underside used as a hotplate.

Lamb Rogan Josh was a firm favourite and nothing that could be rushed, so I began by frying off the meat and spices I'd set to marinade the day before. Once ready, I shifted what I decided to call 'the Beast' over to the nice collection of coals and sank into my chair. The smell was already divine, but with hours to go yet for the fullest flavour and softest, melt-in-the-mouth meat.

I cast a guilty glance at Anxious who was in a mood and huffing as he sat, vibing me from beside the campervan. He was not a fan of spicy food, but I knew he wouldn't sulk for long because he wasn't one to hold a grudge.

"How about if you just have naan?"

Anxious looked over at the simmering pot, groaned loudly, nodded his head in agreement, then came over and lay at my feet, the grudge relinquished.

Smiling, I sipped on an ice-cold beer and relaxed. Evenings like this, where the sun was still high, the air now warm and pleasant after the sweltering heat of earlier, and with all I needed to hand, made me thankful for my new life and the decision I'd made. It was, without doubt, the best thing for me. Min too.

I forced myself to think of something else. Dwelling on the past led to nothing but heartache. It was the present that was the only important thing.

I dropped my beer into the cup holder as I heard footsteps and turned to see Erin coming down the garden. Standing, I waved and shouted, "Hi."

Anxious yipped when he spied her, then raced over, sure to hop and hold his 'poorly' leg up.

"Oh, you poor thing! Is it still hurting, Anxious?" asked Erin as she bent and ruffled his back.

Anxious sat and lifted his injured leg higher, even adding a pitiful whimper.

"Don't let him fool you," I tutted. "He just walked halfway down and back up the castle road, so he's not that bad."

"Anxious, are you playing pretend?" asked Erin with a muffled giggle.

Anxious wagged his tail and trotted back to me, seemingly now cured of all that ailed him.

"He'll do anything for a cuddle," I laughed.

"Am I disturbing you? I don't want to intrude."

"No, of course not. Thanks for letting me stay. It's a beautiful spot, and makes a change from campsites or pub car parks. Do you want a drink?"

"No thanks, I'm good. But you go ahead."

I retrieved my beer and we stood by the fire, although not too close as we certainly didn't need the heat.

"Everything okay?" I asked, noting her frown and the way she was tugging at her ear, the chains and rings tinkling.

"I guess," Erin shrugged, "but it's been one helluva weird day. I can't get my head around any of it. It's like a play. As though I'm watching this happen but I'm in the audience. I feel out of it, as though life's pretend. Does that make sense?"

"Sure. It's too out-of-the-ordinary. Too wild to wrap your head around. How is everyone at the practice?"

"Coping. Just. Ollie's distraught, Aggie's louder than ever, and Pip's still calming down. I'm numb. The police came back, and we went through things again with them, but so far they have no leads. They spoke to the pet owners again, and anyone they can think of, and they heard about Pip's performance as apparently that snake, Leo, reported her. The detective told me they had spoken to him earlier, too, and he didn't have an alibi for when we were attacked, but they don't think he did it."

"Why not?"

"They wouldn't say, but I'm guessing they have a reason. Or maybe they don't think someone like him could do such a thing. He's a respectable part of the community and all that nonsense."

"I saw him earlier," I admitted. "And followed him."

"Max, that's dangerous!"

"Not really, it isn't. And guess what?"

"What?" Erin leaned in close, eyes wide, holding her breath.

"He met with a man in his sixties with bowed legs, thinning hair, wearing a lumberjack shirt. He had a white van."

"That sounds like Aggie's fella. I bet they're in this together."

"That's what I thought, but it's not enough to tell the police. It could have been for anything."

"Maybe, but it's very suspicious. What were they doing?"

"Just talking. Kent seemed angry and was jabbing Leo. Then Leo stormed off. But here's the thing. Leo was very nervous walking through town. He kept looking over his shoulder and was very stressed."

"His accomplices are after him, maybe?" Erin teased the frayed hem of her striking red and white striped T-shirt, the numerous chains and pendants around her neck jangling. She had a definite punk vibe going on, especially with the ripped jeans and Doc Martens.

"You look so different out of work clothes."

"Thanks! Yeah, we tone it down for the job, just wear basic gear and white jackets to look professional, but I like what I like so change as soon as I can."

"Is Rhys home yet?"

"Nah, and he most likely won't be. He likes the pub, and often eats there, or might be at a mate's house. We get on well, but only because mostly I have the place to myself." Erin laughed, but I detected a nervousness too.

"What is it? There's something you aren't telling me."

"Max, it's... Oh, nothing," Erin sighed, still teasing the hem.

"I know we only just met, but I am a friend. Has something happened?"

"What if it was Leo and Kent?"

"They'll go to jail."

"But think of poor Aggie. She really does dote on him. It will break her heart."

"Maybe it isn't her husband, or maybe it isn't either of them. But we have to do the right thing if we discover it was them. You understand that, right?"

"Yes, of course. Poor Aggie. Oh, I forgot to say, the detective let me in on a secret. Promise to keep it to yourself."

"Of course."

"You know we were talking about smoke bombs, or smoke grenades they called them?"

"Yes."

"And that you can buy them anywhere?"

"Sure."

"They found one out in the car park that hadn't gone off. It must have been dropped."

"Okay."

"And they looked up the brand. It's not one you can buy just anywhere. It's local. From a paintball place up the road. It's less than a mile away. It had their company name on it."

"That's great news! A proper clue. And the detective told you? How come?"

"Because he knows my family. He used to go to school with my dad. He wasn't going to say, but when I got upset and said they'd never find out who did it, or prove it was Leo, he told me to cheer me up. They're most likely already there trying to find out things, but this is good, right?"

"Very. Maybe we should go too?"

"How about tomorrow morning? If I call Ollie, he won't mind me going in late."

"Then it's a date."

"It is?" Erin raised an eyebrow, but didn't seem like she'd mind if it was.

"Um, no. Not that you aren't lovely, and very pretty, but I told you about my ex-wife, didn't I?"

"Yes, but you said you weren't together."

"We aren't, but I'm hoping that in a year we will be."

"And in the meantime?" she asked, head angled coyly. When I didn't say anything, Erin sniggered and punched my arm playfully. "I'm just teasing, Max. I'm not saying you aren't my type, because you are, and I love the long hair and those blue eyes of yours are gorgeous, but it's so sweet you're waiting for your ex. That's cute."

"Um, thanks, I think. I never thought of it as cute or sweet. Maybe sad and desperate, but not sweet."

"It's not sad, it's brilliant. A second chance at a future with the love of your life. You saving yourself, not wanting to mess it up by fooling around with sexy, young punk girls. You're a true gent."

"Thanks. Again, I think," I laughed.

"And besides, I'm too young for you."

"You're right, you are."

With the slightly awkward silence that follows such a conversation stretching out too long, we both burst into laughter and the tension dissolved.

"Oh, I have that list you wanted. Everyone whose pets were taken are from Harlech, so they'll be easy to track down. I wrote down the names, addresses, and phone numbers. Ollie said it was okay, but I checked with them first and they'll be expecting you tomorrow. It's best to call ahead though." Erin handed me the list.

"Thanks. Maybe one of them will shed some light on this." I took a quick look then stowed it in the campervan.

"What's cooking? You're a chef, right?"

"Yes, but I've put the fancy stuff behind me and it's one-pot cooking every night if I can manage it. Tonight it's Rogan Josh. You're welcome to join us."

"Us?" frowned Erin.

"Me and Anxious. Sorry, I'm used to saying us."

"I thought maybe you were expecting company."

"No, just me and the starving dog. He's not a fan of curry, hence the sad puppy eyes."

We both turned to watch Anxious staring desolately at the bubbling pot. He noticed us so held up his paw and whined.

Laughing, Erin said, "Are you sure? Don't feel like you have to."

"It will be nice to have the company. Sit, relax."

I retrieved the other chair and we hung out, chatting and laughing whilst dinner simmered. Erin helped with the rice, and was in charge of the naan while I dished up, then we tucked in, while Anxious had naan with his dog food, every so often lifting his paw and glancing over his shoulder so we wouldn't forget how courageous he was.

After seconds, and with bulging bellies, we cleaned up the kitchen, then Erin said her goodbyes.

"How about a drive to the beach?" I asked Anxious.

He was all ears, and keen to go, so I backed off the levelling ramps and sorted out the gate then we were off. It was a short drive through Harlech then onto the main road, before turning off and driving to a car park the other side of the dunes that separated us from the sea. Like many other Welsh coastal towns, there was a golf course and the path leading to the beach bisected it, so we kept our heads down and hurried up the dunes for fear of getting clobbered by a ball, then it was down the other side and onto the sand.

"Wow, this is huge," I whistled, impressed by the depth of the beach and how far it stretched either side.

We took our time walking to the water, no flinger with me today as Anxious couldn't run, but he was happy enough to trot alongside me and sniff at the seaweed. I had a paddle, but Anxious was sensible and remained out of the water to keep his bandage dry, but I did realise my mistake and regretted coming as he'd get sand under the bandage which would be sore. I removed it, and he was instantly happier, so it must have been causing him trouble.

A long, leisurely walk with plenty of sitting between stretches meant we were out for well over an hour soaking up that special time of day when only a few people remained as the sun sank low over the sea.

Both tired, I tracked back up the dunes with Anxious in my arms, through the golf course, then I drove us home. Back in town, I decided to park on the street and take a look at Kent's van from earlier. Maybe it would still be there and I could look through the window.

Anxious was exhausted, though, so I left the windows open and went alone, ducking into the alley like a thief in the night. The van was gone, but Leo's car was in the same spot, hemmed in on all sides by other vehicles, so I checked there was nobody around and walked over casually. The black BMW was close to the high wall, so I decided to go around the other side where I'd be less likely to be spotted, then stopped dead in my tracks.

Gasping, I pulled out my phone, dialled a number I had used more in the last few weeks than my entire life up to that point, and when I was put through to the police, I said, "Hello, my name is Max Effort. I'm in Harlech, behind the sweet shop next to a black BMW. There's been a murder.

It's a vet called Leo. Can you come soon, please? I think I know who did it."

I hung up after answering a few more questions, and could already hear the wail of sirens in the distance.

Chapter 7

It was dark by the time I unlocked the gate at Erin and Rhys', and I almost forgot to close it behind me.

Forgoing the ramps, I parked as level as I could and slumped into my chair. I'd given the police all the information I could, telling about the meeting I'd witnessed earlier, even following Leo and that I'd suspected he was the culprit as he didn't have an alibi for the murder of Riley at the vets.

What I was told was that I shouldn't be snooping and to leave it to the professionals, but at least they thanked me for being honest. I was reminded to be careful as there was a killer on the loose. Eventually, I was allowed to go, but warned to get in touch if I planned on leaving. I had no intention of going anywhere. I'd made a promise and would stick to it.

Worried I'd caused trouble for Aggie, although if her husband was involved that wasn't my fault, I nevertheless thought it best to inform Erin who could explain to her, so I went up to the house and knocked. She answered after a while, looking groggy—she'd clearly been in bed. I broke the news about Leo being dead, stabbed like Riley the nurse, and she was beyond shocked.

"So it definitely wasn't him then?"

"Maybe, maybe not. If he was in this with Kent, then Kent could have killed him. But Leo could have still been involved with things. That does seem unlikely now though." I explained about telling the police, and she went inside to call Aggie then returned a few minutes later. I'd refused to go inside as I was so hot and bothered and needed the fresh air.

"The police took Kent in for questioning, but Aggie swears he was with her all evening. If Leo's death was recent, it couldn't be him."

"It was recent. My guess was less than an hour ago, and that's what the police confirmed. The, er, the blood was very fresh," I said hurriedly, not wanting to go into too much detail.

"Then that's good. Poor Aggie. I told her about you seeing Kent with Leo this morning, and she said Kent had told her earlier."

"What was it about?"

"Apparently, Leo had tracked him down because he wanted him to pass a message on to Aggie to tell her not to let Pip run wild. But mostly, he was looking for protection."

"Protection?"

"Yeah. I told you about Kent's history, and everyone knows what he was like. Leo wanted him to protect him. Said someone was after him, and he thought he was next. He believed his practice would be targeted like Ollie's, and wanted Kent to be his bodyguard. Kent told him to shove it."

"So they weren't friends?"

"No way. Leo doesn't have friends. He wanted protection, and it looks like he needed it."

"It really does. Look, I'm sorry about this. It's a lot to take in."

"Max, you have nothing to be sorry about. You didn't do it. Are we still on for tomorrow? Going to the paintball place? Please? This is more important than ever now. We have to find who's doing this, and we have to do it fast. Anyone could be next."

"Just lock your doors and make sure the windows are secured. Is Rhys home?"

"Yeah, but he's crashed out and snoring. Didn't even hear the doorbell."

"A few too many, eh?"

"Same as usual," sighed Erin.

"Then be careful."

"You too, Max. Do you want to stay in the house? We have plenty of room."

"No, I'm fine, but thank you for the offer. I'll keep the campervan locked up tight. And I have Anxious. He may be small, but he's ferocious if he needs to be. A right ankle biter."

"I bet he is. Goodnight, Max. And thank you for coming to tell me. You're a decent guy."

"No problem. See you tomorrow."

Back at the van, I cleaned Anxious' stitches, which were healing nicely, then applied Savlon and wrapped his leg in a fresh bandage. He was very brave and just buried his head in my lap while I treated him, then perked up instantly when he had a biscuit.

Once that was done, I ensured everything was cleared away outside, placed the silver foil thing—I still didn't know what they were called—over the front window to stop the light and heat, then we got inside our little home. I closed the curtains, locked up, cursed forgetting to sort out the bed in advance yet again, but managed it like a pro, and soon we were snuggled down.

Concerned I'd be afraid sleeping in a strange place full of unfamiliar sounds, not knowing who might be outside the camper, it came as a pleasant surprise to discover the reality was different. I felt safe in here, protected, and not in danger. After all, when you went camping you were only a thin piece of fabric away from the outside and nothing ever happened. We had steel and glass and locks, so what could happen beyond me getting gassed out by Anxious' noxious farts, of which there were many, and was why I kept a small window open.

Knowing I wouldn't sleep, I read a fun cozy mystery I'd had my eye on for a while, and was soon sucked into the story. With Anxious whimpering in his sleep beside me, I was as happy as any man could be. Lost in a world of another person's imagination, yet somehow it feeling like it was mine as I conjured images of the colourful characters.

After an hour, I still couldn't sleep, and was tempted to get dressed and go for a walk around the town. Would that be a foolish thing to do with a murderer on the loose? Yes, it would. Very irresponsible. Instead, I fought Anxious for the covers, pulled them up high, and shut my eyes again.

I don't know how long it took me to drift off, but just as I did, a godawful banging startled me awake and set Anxious to barking. A dog shouting a warning in a small campervan when he's right beside your ear is a sure way to burst an eardrum, but that was the least of my worries as I sat bolt upright and the ominous and insistent thudding began again.

"Max, are you in there?"

"Min?" I called, relief washing over me as I shook my head. "Is that really you?"

"Yes, of course. Sorry it's so late."

Anxious' barking turned to yipping with excitement, the high pitch not doing my ears any favours, so I crawled out of bed and fumbled a light on, half-blinding myself in the process.

With Anxious clawing at the door, pining, I unlocked it and he launched at the shadowy figure of Min.

"Hey, boy, good to see you too," beamed Min as she held the crazed pooch in her arms and he licked her face, manic.

"You gave me a start. I thought I was under attack," I laughed, pleased to see her but surprised too.

"Sorry. I know it's late, but I just had to come." She stroked Anxious' head and asked, "How are you doing? Were you very brave?"

Remembering he was meant to be poorly, Anxious ceased his licking and held up his paw, mournful, and with his ears down.

"Oh, you poor thing. I bet you were very scared, weren't you?"

"He wasn't too happy about it, but then we had other things on our mind. They fixed him up after everything settled down, and he got plenty of attention from everyone."

"We'll talk about that later. I'm just glad you're both okay. Should we go inside?"

I leaned forward and we exchanged a brief peck on the cheek, then I stood back, crouching in the campervan, both of us suddenly rather awkward.

"Look at us! We're like two strangers," I teased. "Let me come out. I'll stoke the fire and get the chairs."

"Yes, sorry. I never know whether I should hug and kiss you or shake your hand," Min chuckled, that unmistakable glint in her eye of mischief and good humour at her own actions.

"Kissing and hugging sounds good to me," I said, then instantly regretted it.

Min smiled warmly, both of us aware I was joking but not joking, her feeling the same.

Anxious looked from me to her, clearly knowing better than both of us what should be done, so he licked her happily and broke the awkwardness like he always did. We both giggled as she set him down and he wandered off, presumably to have a pee while he had the chance.

I stoked up the dying fire and fed it some kindling. It caught instantly, so I added a few larger pieces, set up the chairs, and put the kettle on while Min stood over the fire, rubbing her hands together.

Once the coffee was made, I settled into the chair with Min beside me. Anxious lay between us, sighing with utter contentment. Our family was complete once more, if just for a while.

"You look beautiful with the glow of the fire highlighting you hair. I love the new style. It's shorter, but suits you.

Min put a hand to her curly, sandy-blond hair, orange highlights dancing as the fire crackled. "Thanks. I fancied a change. Are you sure you like it? It's still quite long, but it's easier to handle."

"It looks beautiful. So do you."

"And how about you? Your hair grows so fast. I only saw you a few weeks ago, but it's really growing out."

"It'll be down to my knees in no time," I said with a wink. "Min, what are you doing here in the middle of the night?"

"I know it's silly, but I was worried about you both." Min tugged at her lip like she always did when she was worried or feeling rather self-conscious, her blue eyes catching the light of the fire as she looked into mine. She knew me so well that Min could read my emotional state with a glance.

"As you can see, we're both fine."

"I knew you would be, but I had to come anyway. I can't stand to think of something happening to either of you."

"You know that we're both capable men. Okay, man and dog. Anxious got fixed up no problem, although he's been milking it ever since. It's been a crazy day, that's for sure, but you know me."

"Tough, capable, handsome."

"No need to stop there," I teased. "Anything else? How about suave, sophisticated, and sexy?"

"Don't push your luck, mister," she warned with a warm, intimate smile that made my heart ache with regret and longing.

"Min, you know these things keep happening around me, so I'm learning to take it all in my stride. But yeah, it was pretty wild. The waiting room filled with smoke. They used smoke grenades. It was chaos with dogs barking and everyone shouting. I was in the small room. What do they call them?"

"The treatment or consultation room?"

"Yes, that's it! I think it's either. Anyway, I was in there with the vet, Ollie, he owns the practice, when we heard it start. Smoke everywhere, everyone screaming, then the nurse, Pip, came from the back and opened windows and as the smoke cleared we found the other nurse, Riley, dead. He was stabbed. People had been hit, most likely with bats, and the animals were stolen. Only one dog was still there, the rest were gone."

"That's insane! They stole the animals?"

"They did. Min, I know I told you that, but there's more now. I took Anxious to the beach this evening and on the way back I went to check something out and found another man dead."

"Max, how do you keep finding these bodies?"

"I'm just lucky, I guess," I said, shrugging.

"More like unlucky. Do you know who he is? Was he killed the same way?"

It took a while to explain the events of the day and how I'd thought it might be Leo, the other vet, but that now it seemed unlikely, or if he was involved there was certainly someone else, too, and Min just listened and asked appropriate questions. She'd always been good at listening, never interrupting unnecessarily, able to wait until she had the full story to offer her opinions, and this was no different.

"It sounds to me like someone has it in for vets."

"It could be, but they didn't go after Ollie. They killed the nurse."

"Mistaken identity? With that much smoke, even if they wore night vision goggles, they wouldn't be able to see much."

"Not much, but enough. They most likely had no idea who they were stabbing, you're right, but could make out the shapes of people. Their aim was good enough to give Aggie and Erin a whack on the head, but to be honest it happened so fast, and it was so confusing, that there's no way to know what they were really doing there."

"Beyond taking the animals. That was definitely part of the plan, wasn't it?"

"It must have been. That's why they hit everyone. To ensure they weren't holding on to their pets."

"But why take a cat? And stealing dogs is risky. They could have been bitten. Selling them on won't be easy, if that's the idea. You'd get, what, a few hundred for the lot if you were lucky?"

"Apparently, the tortoise is valuable, and quite rare, but you're right, it makes no sense. Now there are two bodies, a lot of very upset people, and I know for a fact Aggie will be baying for my blood because I told the police I'd seen her husband talking to the dead vet this afternoon."

"You did the right thing. You have to give the police information like that. You don't owe any of them anything. If he's innocent, they'll release him."

"I'm sure you're right. But I doubt he'll be happy about this."

"Max, you saw him talking to a man who was murdered, and he has a reputation. Of course you did the right thing. Can I put more wood on the fire? I'm a bit cold. I didn't bring a coat, and it's cooler than I expected."

"Let me. And I'll get you something warm. Or we can snuggle up?" I hinted, eyebrows dancing playfully.

"In your dreams."

"Sorry, I know I shouldn't keep acting this way, but I can't help it."

"It's fine. If you didn't, I'd think there was something wrong. Max, we know each other really well, so don't make this weird by pretending to be someone you aren't. We both know where we stand, which is best friends for the foreseeable future, and like we discussed, we'll see where we are in a year. How we feel."

"You know how I feel now, and that won't change."

"No, but we're still going to wait!" she teased.

"I'll get you a blanket."

After getting the fire roaring, I took the still-warm blanket off the bed and wrapped it around Min's shoulders, unable to stop myself taking a cheeky sniff of her hair from behind.

"Are you sniffing me again?" she teased. "You know that's weird, right?"

"I was not sniffing you!" I said, indignant. "And even if I was, it's not weird."

"It so is," she laughed, our eyes meeting as I stood by the fire.

"Maybe a little," I admitted, grinning.

"What are you so upbeat about?"

"I'm pleased to see you, like always. And look at him."

We studied Anxious, curled up tight next to Min now, having shifted over to feel her presence.

"He's so cute. I bet he's had lots of extra treats today, especially if he showed people his bandage."

"He's been playing on it all afternoon. We were sat on a wall by the castle and you should have seen him."

"Was the castle nice?"

"It looks amazing, but we didn't go inside."

"Maybe we can check it out tomorrow? Although, I suppose it is tomorrow. It's early morning already."

"Don't you have to get back for work?"

"I'll stay for the day, if that's okay? Then go home."

"Great! Yes, absolutely. We'll have a nice time, just the three of us." I frowned, remembering that I had plans.

"What's wrong?"

I explained about going to the paintball place with Erin, and Min said she'd tag along, then we could play it by ear, so we were all set.

We talked for a while longer, but were both exhausted, so I let Min take the bed and I remained in the chair, warmed by the fire and comforted by knowing she was only a few steps away.

Right where she belonged.

Chapter 8

Anxious did a double-take when Min opened the campervan door in the morning and stepped out.

As happy as him, I said, "Yes, she's really here. It wasn't a dream."

Anxious lifted his poorly leg to show her, and I swear he winked at me!

"Oh, you poor thing! Does it still hurt, my brave little trooper?"

He whined, then sat wagging happily as Min fussed over him.

"Don't let him fool you. He's fine now, and even Ollie said it was minor."

"But look at his little sad face," cooed Min, sitting on the edge of the campervan floor and playing with the happy dog.

"We should get him into films. He's a great actor."

"Don't be so mean," said Min, smiling at me. "Gosh, you look like you need a few more hours sleep. Sorry I woke you last night."

"It's fine. I'm glad you came. And Anxious sure is."

I made coffee and we sorted ourselves out, then Erin arrived just before nine. She wore a startling green and black striped, long-sleeved T-shirt today, with torn jeans and her boots, and it was obvious Min wasn't prepared for how she looked. They sized each other up, clearly decided they could be friends, and after I explained why Min was here, Erin seemed to relax.

"What?" I asked, as both women studied me.

"Why are you smiling?" asked Min suspiciously.

"You look weird," noted Erin.

"I do not look weird, and I'm not smiling," I countered, noting I was grinning.

"Ah, I get it," said Erin.

"You do?" I asked.

"Yeah. Min, cards on the table?" said Erin.

"Sure. What's this about?"

"Max and I had a thing yesterday."

"We did not!" I stammered.

"A bit of flirting. Gah, this is embarrassing. He's kind of hot, and I fancy him a little, but he put me straight, said he was holding out for you. Isn't that cute?"

"Very," said Min slowly, raising an eyebrow.

"And I said I was too old for her," I added hurriedly.

"He is quite old," admitted Erin. "But still hot."

"He is hot," agreed Min.

"Ha!" was all I managed, feeling uncomfortable with the attention.

"But he's a bit of a muppet, right?" teased Erin.

"That's one thing we can definitely agree on."

"So we cool?" asked Erin. "I didn't know the deal with you guys, but now I do I'll keep my hands off."

"I don't own him," said Min. "Max can do what he wants."

"I can?" I asked lamely. "Um, you aren't dating, are you?" My heart hammered as beads of sweat popped up all over my body as I waited for the dreaded answer.

"Max, of course not! We might not be together that way, but no, I am not dating. I wouldn't do that to you."

"Even though you're divorced?" asked Erin. "You haven't seen anyone in over a year?"

"No, and it will stay that way."

"Good," I gushed, sighing with relief.

Min smiled sweetly and my heart slowed, and I couldn't even begin to hide my sense of relief.

"You guys are adorable!" laughed Erin. "So, we cool?"

"We're cool," said Min, then she hugged Erin and winked at me over her shoulder. "But I can see the attraction. You're very pretty."

"Thank you."

We stood there shuffling our feet and looking everywhere but at each other, then we laughed and it was like we'd known Erin for years.

"Let's get this show on the road," I suggested.

"Why are we going to the paintball place again?" asked Min.

"Because the police told Erin that the smoke grenades came from there. They will have already been, but it won't hurt for us to check it out."

"That's right," agreed Erin. "Oh, and I spoke to everyone from the practice this morning. Aggie's husband was released in the early hours. He had an alibi. He was at home with her when Leo was killed, and they've given him the all clear."

"That's good. Was she cross with me? Is he?"

"Relax, Max, it's all good. They both thought you did the right thing. Kent was annoyed at being accused, but it's understandable."

"How's Ollie?"

"Stunned. And worried this isn't over. We need to find who did it."

"That's what we're trying to do," I said.

"Then come on, let's go," said Min. "I've only got today, so it would be nice to help find the killer and retrieve the missing animals. Are we going to visit the owners?"

"I'd like to, but don't you have work, Erin?"

"I can only spare enough time to visit the paintball site. Maybe you two could call on the owners? I'd like to come, but Ollie needs me. He's allowed to open up today, so they'll be short-staffed without me. Not that we expect anyone will come after what happened."

"Sounds like a plan."

Erin sorted out the gate while I drove through, then I followed her directions and headed into the hills to a paintball site called, not very imaginatively, Paintball in the Hills.

I drove through what amounted to a fictitious war zone, everything splattered in paint every colour of the rainbow. Old buses, wooden towers, tree houses, gigantic tyres, and all manner of obstacles hidden amongst the forest of pine trees. It looked like it must be great fun to spend a few hours running around, hiding and shooting at people without the risk of injury.

"Have you ever played?" I asked Erin.

"Of course! Haven't you?"

"No, but I wish I had."

"What about you, Min?" Erin called from the back.

"Never. Is it dangerous?"

"No, they supply you with masks and the gear. It's exhausting, because you get really into it. There's paint flying everywhere, they use the smoke grenades, there are all different colours of smoke, too, and if you have enough friends you can be on the same team playing against other people. It's awesome!"

"Do you do it often?" I asked as I parked.

"No. Haven't been for a few years. I've only done it a couple of times anyway. It's quite expensive, and I'm not rolling in cash."

"What about the others?"

"No idea. But Rhys loves it."

"Who's Rhys again?" asked Min.

"That's my brother. He fixed the camper for Max."

"Right, yes. He plays?"

"He comes now and then with his mates."

Min and I exchanged a look as we got out, but said nothing.

"Hey, I saw that. Don't go getting any ideas about Rhys. He works hard and plays hard, but he's no killer. And why would he do such a terrible thing?"

"We didn't mean anything by it, Erin," I said.

"Sorry," said Min.

"Just being thorough, eh?" she teased.

"Yes, which we need to be. But there are no accusations here. We were just thinking out loud." I considered my words, then added, "Um, out loud, but in our heads."

They both stared at me like I'd grown another arm, but I refused to say another word as I was feeling rather strange with them both here.

Three men came over to see what we wanted, but the moment I began to explain, two of them left, grumbling about the police and that they weren't in the mood for more questions.

"Sorry about them," said a grizzly man in his fifties with wild, long brown hair streaked with grey at the sides, a beard down to his chest, and wearing army fatigues. "The police swarmed us and we worried they'd shut us down. We have nothing to hide, though, so I guess you better ask away. I know Erin, but who are you? I'm Dai."

"Another Dai?" I asked.

"How'd you mean? It's the most common name in the country."

"Right, of course." I made the introductions, and Anxious showed Dai his poorly leg so got a biscuit. He trotted off happily and rested by the pine-clad office.

"I think I just got played," Dai grumbled, smiling as Anxious tucked in.

"I think you might be right," I agreed, wondering if Anxious had done it to make us relax. He was a smart one, no doubt.

"Um, hang on a mo. I just need to finish what I was doing. I'll be there now in a minute."

When he returned to the office, Min asked, "Be there now in a minute?" eyebrows raised.

"It's a Welsh thing," explained Erin.

"Hi, sorry about that. Told you I wouldn't be long," said Dai with a wink for Erin and Min.

Both tittered like young girls for some reason, but I didn't understand why.

"What did the police have to say?" asked Erin. "You don't mind talking to us, do you? I was there when it happened. So was Max."

"That must've been rough. I don't mind, but it'll have to be quick. We've got a booking at half past. They'll be here any minute."

"We'll be quick," said Erin. "So, what did the police say?"

"Just asked about the smoke grenades," shrugged Dai. "I'll tell you what I told them. We go through literally hundreds a week. People come from all over for a fun few hours, or half a day, and we supply them with the gear and a few hundred paintballs, but we sell extras. Most people run out of the paintballs so buy more, and we sell the smoke grenades too. It's madness here sometimes," he chuckled.

"But can people come and buy them without playing?" I asked.

"Sure, and we sell the guns, goggles, and protection too. Pretty much anything paintball. Why?"

"Just wondered if someone came and bought the smoke grenades without playing."

"Maybe. We're the main seller in the area, and lots of guys, women, too, have their own set-ups on farms, places like that. A few of them get together and have mini battles. So, yeah, we do good business."

"Can you think of anyone who acted suspiciously recently when they bought grenades?"

"Mate, who doesn't look suspicious? Let's get real here," he said, checking we weren't being overheard. "It's mostly guys playing war, right? Some people are really into this, and some are way too into it, if you get my drift. Which means a lot of the guys who buy from us are suspicious as hell!" Dai winked at the ladies again. They both giggled. What was with that?

"Do you have names and addresses?"

"Course not! And if I did, I wouldn't give them to you. It's their business. I'm not being funny, but that's an invasion of their privacy."

"It was worth a try," I said.

"Sure. You don't ask, you don't get. But you asked, and you ain't getting. Plus, I don't keep those kind of records. Shops don't write down the names and addresses of their customers."

"Before we go," I said, "is there anything you can think of that might help us?"

"The same thing I told the police. Whoever it was, they had state-of-the-art night vision goggles. They most likely had serious military kit. I've been around the smoke grenades a lot, and I know for a fact that in a confined space even with IR it would be tough to see a damn thing. They had proper kit, not stuff that costs a few hundred, but the high-end gear that works properly. Army stuff."

"And do you sell that?"

"No fear! Nobody would buy it. This is for people to play at war, not actual soldiers. It's about fun. A way to let loose, burn off the pent-up energy, frustration, that kind of thing. You should try it some time."

"Maybe we will," I said. "Thanks for your time."

"No problem, and I hope you figure this out. It's not good for anyone to have some nutter running around killing people. Especially if it leads the police and nosy buggers to my door." With a final wink eliciting another mystifying giggle from the ladies, he turned and went into the office.

"Why were you giggling?" I asked, nonplussed.

"We weren't," they chorused.

"What? What's happening?"

"He was cute," said Erin, shrugging.

"He was?"

"He was," confirmed Min. "But don't worry, you're still our favourite hairy hunk."

"You are," agreed Erin.

"I am?" I asked, smiling so much my face hurt.

"Yes," said Min. She turned to Erin and explained, "I've told Max he's a handsome guy, with a great personality, and fun, too, lots of times, but he doesn't see it."

"That's the true sign of a great catch," said Erin seriously.

"I am here, you know?" I sighed, shaking my head.

"We know!" they chorused happily.

Anxious returned to see what the noise was about, no sign of a limp, so it was time to take Erin to work. We might not have learned much, but we had learned something, so it had been worth making the trip.

I slowed as we approached the clinic, and we gasped.

"I was expecting it to be deserted," said Erin.

"Me too. What's going on?" I asked.

"No idea. But we never get this many people. Maybe something else has happened?"

We hurried over to the entrance just as Aggie and her husband, Kent, emerged, sweating and looking nervous.

"What's the matter?" asked Erin.

"It's a madhouse in there!" boomed Aggie, causing me to wince and Min to jump back, startled.

"How'd you mean? "

"I mean, the place is overrun. I had to come out for some air. I'm so hot." Aggie glared at me, so I smiled back, trying to show I didn't hold a grudge against her husband, who was yet to speak.

"Why are there so many people? Is there a problem?" Erin nodded to Kent, who just grunted, before she turned back to Aggie.

"It's because of what happened to Leo. They closed the other practice. A corporate policy thing, apparently. They won't risk getting into trouble for anything, so shut it down. Everyone's come here. Mind you," crowed Aggie, her voice getting louder if anything, "there are only a couple of ill pets. Everyone else has just come to gossip. But we got a few new sign-ups for the medical cover plan we offer, and my Kent has been great helping out. He dropped me off then stayed because of all the people."

"That's sweet of you," said Erin. "Oh, this is Max and Min. And that's Anxious."

"What's anxious?" he asked, his voice surprisingly mellow and friendly.

"The dog. It's his name," I offered. "He isn't, but it's his name."

"Isn't what?" asked Kent with a suspicious frown as he leaned forward and peered at me intently.

"His demeanour isn't anxious, but his name is."

"Is he trying to be funny?" Kent asked Erin.

"No, I don't think so. Are you?"

"Absolutely not. If I was, you'd know it," I said.

"Not always," giggled Min. "Hi, nice to meet you both. Aggie, was it?"

"Yes, that's me!" screeched Aggie, shaking Min's hand happily and giving me another scowl.

"Sorry about the trouble I think I might have got you into," I told Kent. "I saw you with Leo, and when I found him dead you can understand why it seemed suspicious."

"No hard feelings, young un. I would have done the same thing. He was a vile man, but I'm no killer. Right by where I'd parked my van earlier, too, which was bad luck for me, even worse for him."

"What do you think he was doing there?"

"Probably just going home," he shrugged. "Or wanted to nick my tools to protect himself. Daft numpty should have stayed away."

"Yes, well, that's enough of that!" said Aggie. "I need to sit down. I'm exhausted already."

"You take the load off," said Erin. "I'll go and take over. How is everyone? Are Ollie and Pip okay?"

"Yes, fine. Shaken, and stressed, but fine."

With that, Ollie emerged looking utterly freaked out.

"You're all here," gasped Ollie, holding on to the doorframe to steady himself.

"What happened to you?" I asked.

"Max, it's just intense in there. There are so many people, and everyone is asking questions. To be blunt, I'm terrified someone's going to kill me. I don't think we should have opened. What were the police thinking? They should know better."

"I'm guessing they assumed everyone would stay away, but wanted to let you help any animals that needed it. Maybe you should close? It could be dangerous. For everyone."

"Don't be daft," grumbled Kent. "They've already been here. No way will they return. Not with so many people. And besides, you don't want to turn away the business. Nice little earner for you, eh, Ollie? You sure this wasn't down to you?"

"How dare you!" snapped Ollie, his cheeks flushing.

"And unless everyone's forgotten," I interrupted, "Ollie was with me and Anxious."

"Was he? Aggie said you came out first, but Ollie was still in the interrogation room."

"It's not an interrogation room!" hissed Ollie. "It's an examination room."

"Oh, yeah, I forgot," said Kent with a sneer.

I couldn't get a handle on Kent. One minute he was friendly and softly spoken, the next he was full of venom. Did he and Ollie have history? I'd have to ask Erin.

"Anyway," said Kent like he hadn't heard Ollie, "you were in the room while Max came out first. And everyone was screaming but nobody saw anything. Then poor Riley was found by Pip. Could have been any of you. Apart from my Aggie and Erin, of course."

"You're just being silly now," stammered Ollie, his colour rising further. "I came out for some air, but it's more foul out here than in there." He turned to me and asked, "How is Anxious? And how are you? Shaken up, I expect, after finding Leo."

"I'm doing okay, and so is Anxious, despite what he says."

"And how are you feeling?" Ollie asked as he squatted next to Anxious, clearly finding comfort with him rather than having to deal with Kent any longer.

Anxious cocked his head, then lifted his poorly paw and whined.

"Don't fall for it," I warned.

"I think we better get you inside and take a look at that," said Ollie.

Anxious dropped his paw and raced around Ollie, showing that there was nothing to see here and no need to be taken into the "interrogation" room.

"Ha! In your face, Anxious!" I laughed as I scooped him up and he whined for real this time. "That will teach you to pretend. Ollie's the doctor, so it's time for your examination."

Ollie nodded, so I turned to Min and asked, "Can you wait out here for five? We won't be long."

"I'll come too. I want to see how he is."

"Sure. I just thought you'd rather wait."

"Why?"

"Because you hate the smell, and it'll be pretty intense."

"Our clinic doesn't smell," roared Aggie.

"Aggie, it really does," corrected Erin. "It's unavoidable. We do our best, but let's face it, it's full of nervous dogs making a mess on the floor."

Kent left as the rest of us entered what can only be described as a smelly madhouse.

Chapter 9

It was easy to see why everyone was so hot and stressed. The temperature was stifling with the amount of people and animals. Dogs were panting, people likewise, as they stood or sat in varying degrees of either fear or boredom.

Erin rushed behind the reception counter and donned her white coat, then smiled as she began to deal with the queue of people who all, seemingly, wanted to register and have their pets looked at. Judging by the snippets of overheard conversation, there was nothing wrong with most animals and everyone had simply come to get the gossip.

Ollie ushered us into the examination room where I placed Anxious on the table and he stood, again showing Ollie that he was fine.

"This will only take a minute, Anxious," soothed Ollie as he removed the bandage and we all craned in to get a look at the stitches. Anxious turned his head away, so Min let him nuzzle into her.

"It's healing nicely. The stitches are dissolvable, so in about a week they'll be gone. The wound's closed up, and it's clean, so there's nothing to worry about."

"That's great," I said.

"You hear that, Anxious?" said Min softly. "You're going to live!"

We exchanged a wink and a smile, so with Anxious wagging happily, I lowered him to the floor and gave him a biscuit.

"Thanks for taking a look at him," I told Ollie.

"My pleasure. It looks like I'm going to have a very busy day, which is unexpected, so wanted to see you guys first. I can't believe Leo's dead. Was it awful?"

"Pretty bad, yes. Ollie, what can be going on here? There must be a link."

"I wish I knew." Ollie gathered up the bandage and binned it, then washed his hands. "I'm feeling very exposed here, and I wish I knew what to do. Do you think it could have been Kent? That man is a nightmare."

"You heard Aggie. He was with her."

"Maybe she's lying. No, don't listen to me. She wouldn't do that. They're both good people, but he gets under my skin. Are you still willing to help?"

"I said I would, and I will."

We explained about the paintball site and what we'd discovered, but Ollie had no idea where you would buy military equipment or who might have done so, and had no new insights into motive or who to question, so it was time for us to go.

"Are you sure you should be open?" asked Min. "Why not close up and wait until this is done? If you're afraid, maybe that's for the best."

"I don't think they'll be after me. I'm just jumpy. There are too many people around, but I'm sure that will ease right off in a few hours. No, I'll keep busy. That's for the best. No time to think about things too much. But please get in touch if you discover anything."

"Sure. We'll visit the pet owners, see if they know anything, and take it from there," I said.

As I opened the door into the waiting room, I got a very intense, almost overwhelming sense of déjà vu. My heart hammered as I fought down a rising tide of panic and gasped.

"You got it too?" asked Ollie. "It's happened every time I open the door. I can still picture the chaos and hear the screams. What are we going to do, Max?"

"We'll find who did this," I said through gritted teeth. Min squeezed my hand and smiled knowingly, so, buoyed by her kindness, I marched into the busy waiting room then straight out of the front door with Anxious by our side.

More cars were arriving, and people were hanging around on the grass, talking excitedly and seemingly unconcerned about the danger.

"Why are they here? I don't get it?" I said to Min.

"They want to see where it happened. It's rather odd, isn't it? It's like a party, not a crime scene."

"I can't believe the police let this happen. It's nuts. Someone could get hurt."

"The killer isn't going to come back. It has to be more than one person, surely?"

"I think you're right. Two people at least. Maybe it was more?"

"That increases the risk though. The less there were involved in this, the less chance of getting caught. Come on, let's get out of here."

Shaking our heads at the morbid curiosity of the locals, we buckled up and I drove into town then parked. The hills were a struggle for Vee, even after Rhys had worked his magic, so we sorted out a route and decided we could visit everyone on foot. The town wasn't large, and only one person lived away from the heart of Harlech, so we could drive to visit them last.

"Are you sure you want to spend your morning traipsing around talking to people?" I asked Min as we headed up the hill.

"Of course. It'll be cool to see the town, and we have to do something. Everyone seems so nice, if odd, and I want to help."

"You got a shock when you met Erin, didn't you?" I teased.

"I did. She's very pretty, and rather wild. She's fun." Min tugged at her lip then smiled and said, "She fancies you."

"Yes, we went through that. No need to make fun of me."

"I'm just playing. Max, you do know that you're a free man, right? I'm not expecting you to do anything on my account. You can do what you want."

"Min, what are you saying? You want me to go off with another woman?" I asked, stopping.

"No, it's just... Gosh, I don't know."

"Be honest. Say what you want to say."

"Then I will!" she snapped. "Don't you dare touch another woman! I know that's a horrid thing to say, but I couldn't bear it. I know we don't owe each other anything, but—"

"Min, I owe you everything. You know how I feel, so don't beat yourself up for not wanting me to get together with someone else. I won't."

"I hadn't considered the fact you might fall for someone. I've been clear about not promising anything with you, haven't I?"

"Yes, you have, and I told you that's fine. That I'll wait."

"But what if we never do get back together? It's so confusing. We're both free agents, but now I'm telling you not to try to build a future for yourself."

"You're my future. You know I want that, but I'm not putting any pressure on you. If you found someone else, I'd hate it, but it's your life and you do what you want."

"And I feel the same way. But I also don't want you to fall for anyone else. What a mess!" Min toyed with her hair and shook her head, clearly feeling awkward.

"I will never do anything to hurt you again. I wouldn't do that."

"But that's so unfair on you. You might miss out on the opportunity to have a life with someone else."

"No, that won't happen."

"Max, I'm so sorry. This is wrong."

"Min, I don't blame you for anything. I don't expect a thing from you, understand? This is my decision, not yours. There's nothing for you to feel bad about. It's my decision."

"Life sure is complicated at times, isn't it?"

"It is, but we're alive, and together for a few hours, so let's try to do some good and help these people."

"Yes, let's. I'm glad I came." Min smiled weakly then nodded.

"Me too."

After a strenuous climb, we found a small cottage nestled into the hill with a tiny front garden and nothing at the rear but rock. I knocked on the door and it opened almost immediately.

"Hi, I'm Max," I told the lady as she smiled. "I called earlier."

"Yes, hello. And you are?"

"I'm Min, a, er, friend," she said, bypassing the need for a lengthy explanation of our relationship.

"Can we come in for a chat? Or should we speak outside?"

"Let's sit in the garden. The cottage is very small, and I'm afraid I've been too upset to tidy up. My poor boy! Oh, what will I do without him?"

"It was a cat, yes?" I asked.

"Yes, my little darling. Sorry, I must look a mess. I haven't even brushed my hair." Ivy tamed her mass of tight brown curls and smoothed down a blue housecoat. She was well-presented with loose linen trousers and a matching dark blouse, but the smell of cat was strong and I was pleased she'd suggested the garden.

Anxious' nose was going haywire as he sniffed Ivy's steps, clearly desperate to mark the territory, but he knew better than that so waited patiently.

Ivy indicated a small white table and matching chairs so we sat and Anxious stuck close, maybe put off by the intensity of the aromas. Ivy was a nervous woman with wandering eyes and thin lips that she pursed repeatedly. Her frown lines were deep and she clearly wasn't a smiler, and I immediately felt like we were wasting our time. It clearly wasn't her. She was rather stooped, and frail, and her hands shook as she clasped them in her lap.

"Is there anything you can tell us about yesterday? Something that might help?"

"I told the police everything I could, but it wasn't much. There was so much smoke, and my lungs aren't what they were. People were shouting, and then there were screams. It was so sudden, and my Percy was wailing."

"Percy is your cat? Is he a special breed?" asked Min softly.

"No, just a regular tabby. I don't know why anyone would take the little dear. He was very afraid and scratched me terribly when I put him in his carrier. We were only there for his yearly jabs. He hates it. Will you get him back? Will you find who did this?" Ivy studied her hands, the red scratches prominent over her bony fingers.

"We'll do our best. What about voices? Did you hear anyone? Do you think it was one person or more?"

"I didn't hear them. The smoke was so dense, and then the carrier was gone. Someone grunted next to me because they must have been hit, but luckily I wasn't. My poor darling will be so scared."

"We'll do whatever we can," I soothed. "Do you live alone? Any family here? Anyone else we should speak to?"

"No, it's just me. Please find Percy. He's my company. I don't feel right without him here. He's always around. He's still young, only three, but he stays close and is a good boy."

"I'm sure he's great company. One final question. Can you think of anyone who might do something like this? Any reason why?"

"Absolutely not! I know there was rivalry between the two practices, but poor Ollie is doing a wonderful job. Everyone thought maybe it was Leo, that sneak, but now he's dead too. What is the world coming to?"

"It's a terrible thing."

We thanked Ivy then took our leave. As we walked to the next address, we both confirmed that Ivy should be ruled out. She was an elderly lady living alone with a cat for company, not a killer capable of stealing animals, committing murder, and running around with military-grade night vision goggles. The idea was ludicrous.

Next was a dog owner. An elderly man who lived with his sick wife in a sprawling bungalow half a mile from town. The dog was a rare Red Setter and only six months old. Their favourite breed. They had another older dog, and the young one was company for her. Both the man and his wife gushed over the breed, lamenting the loss. Again, we promised to do what we could, and asked the same questions, but neither could think of any reason for the killings, and were more concerned about their dog having been sold than anything else.

It was only a short walk to the other dog owner's house, so we hurried to the address, spoke briefly to a polite man, and got nowhere but stressed by the noise of his three Labradors as they tore around the small garden, destroying what little was left of the yellow lawn. Anxious remained by our side, wary, and knowing this was way out of his league. We were polite, asked the appropriate questions, but he had no insights and couldn't understand why on earth anyone would take a young puppy.

The owner of the parrot lived at the bottom of town and across the road amid a haphazard collection of houses, and it was only once we'd got onto level ground that we regretted walking. It was a steep climb back up, and the day was already hot without a cloud in the sky.

"We'll have muscles on our muscles once we get back up there," I noted, looking up at the castle looming large on the hill.

"It'll do us good," said Min, sounding utterly unconvinced. "It's so hot. We need shade. I'm burning up. Did you bring water?"

"No, but I wish I had. Maybe the next owner will offer us a drink."

"I hope so."

The front gardens of the gleaming white houses were open to the pavement, the scrubby grass yellow and struggling under the dry conditions. Hydrangeas were loving it though. Tough varieties suited to the coastal conditions and the salty air. We took the path up to the house and Min knocked, both grateful for the shade from the large overhanging roof.

"Who's that?" asked a high-pitched voice I couldn't decide was male or female.

"It's Max. I called earlier."

"Who's that?" asked the voice again.

Min and I exchanged a shrug, so I repeated. "Max. I called about the missing parrot."

The door opened and a topless man hurriedly stepped outside and pulled the door closed behind him. "Sorry about that," he sighed, his deeply tanned bald head gleaming with sweat. He tried to suck in his belly when he noted Min, but it was a lost cause and we all knew it. Hitching up a pair of grubby denim shorts, he frowned and added, "She gets stuck on repeat sometimes."

"She?" I asked, not following.

"Mrs. Blue Beak."

"That's a strange name for your wife," said Min with a smile for the man, who frowned.

"Wife? I don't have a wife. Oh, sorry, yes, this is rather confusing. It's the female parrot. She's called Mrs. Blue Beak. She's very rare, and very talkative. But sometimes it gets repetitive."

"Ah, that makes sense," laughed Min.

We made our introductions, which, as usual, led to some confusion, then Anthony Mandel invited us inside. As we were about to enter, he suddenly turned and asked, "Will the dog behave?"

"Absolutely. Why?"

"I don't want him eating my parrot."

"He won't eat your parrot," I promised. I turned to Anxious and asked, "Will you eat the parrot?"

Anxious lifted his bandaged paw, looked Anthony in the eye, and whimpered.

"Aw, you poor thing. What happened?"

"He cut his paw, but he's fine now. He's angling for a treat."

"Then let's see what we can rustle up. Hurry inside. I don't want Mrs. Blue Beak to escape."

We slid through the partially opened door, then Anthony closed it hurriedly.

Min, Anxious, and I stopped and gasped as a huge parrot glared, it's head cocked to the side, from it's position on the newel post at the bottom of the stairs.

"Wow, she's huge," I gasped.

"She's forty years old and it took decades for her to reach that size. Mind your fingers. She's friendly, but she likes to nibble."

"Mr. Red Beak?" asked the parrot, cocking her head to the other side.

"She misses him. They were together for a long time. We both miss him. Come through to the kitchen. I was about to make a drink. Do you want one? How about Anxious?"

"We'd love a drink, thank you," said Min, edging around the parrot as it followed us with its eyes.

"Something cold, I'm guessing," said Anthony, sighing as he rubbed at his tanned head. "I'm burning up. Sorry for the lack of clothes, but it's too hot."

"Something cold would be great. And we don't mind what you wear," I said.

The kitchen was vast, dated, but incredibly humid. The impressive trifold doors were closed and there was so much glass that it was hotter than a greenhouse.

"Let me make the drinks then we should go outside. I have to keep everything closed in case Mrs. Blue Beak tries to escape. Normally, she'll be fine and won't fly off, but since we lost Mr. Red Beak she hasn't been herself."

"They bond for life, don't they?" I asked.

"Yes, and she's distraught. Poor thing."

Anthony made everyone a cool glass of lemonade and put a bowl of water down for Anxious, which lapped at eagerly, then we went outside and sat under the shade of a pergola festooned with a grape vine sagging with bunches of dark, juicy orbs.

Once settled, and after a welcome drink, we got down to business.

Anthony was convinced the theft had been about his parrot. The bird was rare, could easily sell for a few thousand pounds to the right buyer, and maybe more if the thieves weren't in any hurry.

"Was your parrot sick?" asked Min.

"No, just a yearly check-up. They're both in fine health, but it's best to get them looked at. I hadn't even been in to see Ollie and now these terrible things have happened. Awful, just awful."

"Did you ever try the other vet?" I asked.

"That idiot? I went there once, just to see, but I felt bad as it was like breaking a trust. I've been going to Ollie's practice for years and years, but thought I'd check the others out. I met that guy, Leo, and we didn't see eye to eye. He didn't have a friendly manner, and rubbed me up the wrong way. Don't know why anyone ever went there, apart from the cost. Leo was doing everything he could to poach Ollie's business, including offering low prices for the first visit, so I guess I got swayed by that." Anthony shrugged, then finished his lemonade.

"Nobody seems to have a good word to say about Leo," noted Min. "Can you think of anyone who might have wanted him dead?"

"Ollie, for a start," laughed Anthony. "And most likely half the people in town. He wasn't well-liked. One of those men nobody could get along with."

"Even though he was the vet? Surely people liked him to use his services?" asked Min.

"Times are tough. People go with cheap. It is what it is."

"But is there anyone who would want him dead for real?" I asked.

"No, not that I know of. Look, let's be honest here. They wanted my parrot, and then they figured they'd get rid of Leo."

"But why? How are they connected?" I pushed.

"Because I bet Leo was in on it. It's obvious, isn't it? Leo would have connections, know who to sell the parrot to for the best money. Get a few extra quid for the tortoise and the dogs and cat maybe, but my bird was priceless!"

"You might be right. Leo would certainly know the right people, but it's hard to imagine someone who cares about animals doing such an unspeakable thing," I said.

"People will do all sorts for money," said Anthony.

We agreed they definitely would. A few minutes later, with the conversation going nowhere, we found ourselves back out on the street, sweltering under the glaring sun, with a worrying climb ahead of us.

"You ready?" I asked Min.

"For lunch, yes," she said, smiling.

"Let's get up to the castle first. I'll treat you to a meal in their restaurant," I promised.

It took a while.

Chapter 10

"I don't think we're the only ones with the same idea," noted Min with a frown as we stood inside the restaurant and marvelled at the volume of visitors.

"I don't care. They have air-con. I'm actually getting goosebumps I'm so cool. It's awesome."

"Isn't it amazing? Let's go and order then see if there are any seats."

The restaurant was a self-service style place perfect for moving plenty of volume without having endless waiting staff. We chose our food and drinks, then were served by stressed staff before paying.

A couple were vacating a table, so we nabbed it quickly and sank into our seats right by the window overlooking the bridge that led from the visitor centre, gift shop, and restaurant combo. A steady stream of people walked past the huge windows and across the bridge, hurrying into the shade the towering remains of Harlech Castle offered.

"When was it built? I haven't had a chance to read about it yet," asked Min.

"The thirteenth century. Apparently, the sea used to be much closer and you could descend steps on the other side to the Irish Sea. Now it's what, a few miles away? Crazy how different it must have looked then. None of the houses below would have been there, and the dunes wouldn't either."

"That's incredible. Are we still going to go and explore?"

"Sure. I promised."

"Let's visit the last pet owner first, then come back. We won't be hurrying then. This is nice." Min took another bite of her chicken and smiled happily.

I tried mine and was pleased to find it was soft, hot, and well-seasoned. "Not bad at all."

For a while, we focused on our food without talking. A comfortable silence born of years of a shared life together. There were no awkward silences, just two people who knew each other better than any other person in the world.

Anxious curled up under the table, one eye open in case any chicken managed to escape our plates. Huffing once he realised he was out of luck, he snuggled his nose right up by his tail and began to snore.

After we'd finished our meal, we took our time over drinks, enjoying the cool air and the company. Discussion soon turned to the people we'd met so far.

"We can rule out the cat owner, and the dog owners, I think," said Min.

"Absolutely. Elderly people who adore their pets but wouldn't be able to do the deed. The owner of the puppy didn't seem suspicious either."

"And I can't picture Anthony running around and stealing animals," said Min, frowning.

"Neither can I. He was a big guy and too nice. He clearly dotes on his parrots. How could he have them in the house like that though? They'd make a mess everywhere. You'd spend all your time cleaning up after them."

"I guess it's better than them being in cages. Did you see the huge one in the living room?"

"Yes, when we were leaving. But I don't think he uses it much. So we rule him out too?"

"We have to. Max, who does this leave us with?"

"Currently, nobody, unless Aggie's covering for her husband and it was him. But she's too caring about animals to be involved in something like this, and she got hit, remember?"

"So that leaves us with nobody. Gosh, how will you figure this out?"

"Something will turn up. At least, I hope it does. It has every other time. I'll keep asking around, talking to people, and see what surfaces."

"You have the right skills for this, so I'm sure you'll figure it out. What are you feeling?"

"Min, it's the weirdest thing. It's like I'm overlooking something blindingly obvious that I've already seen or heard and it's utterly blatant. I know I'm good with details, but this feels different than the other times. I can't put my finger on it, but something's not right."

"Of course it isn't right, silly. Two people have been murdered. The culprit or culprits used smoke grenades and most likely had access to military equipment. And they stole animals. It's utterly bonkers."

"Yes, I know, but there's something else. I'm sure something's either been said, or not been said when it should have been. Sorry, now I'm not even making sense to myself," I chuckled.

"You'll get there. Come on, let's go and visit the last person on the list."

Luckily, it wasn't far back to the campervan, but we were still beat by the time we arrived. Min freshened up while I sorted a few thing out and let Anxious rest in the shade, then I took a turn having a wash and returned to find her waiting outside Vee, smiling.

"What are you so happy about?"

"I'm just happy. This has been fun. I know it's serious, and I feel for everyone, but these mysteries are exciting. You have to admit that."

"True, they are, and I keep feeling bad about being intrigued by them. But I've come to realise this is how detectives and the police feel. They want to help people, but they also enjoy the thrill. Murder is truly terrible, but by stopping the killers you're doing a terrific thing, so you can't help feeling good too. It's a weird predicament to be in."

"Nothing wrong with happy vibes whilst helping others. Shall we go?"

Anxious would have preferred to sleep the rest of the day away, but he'd rather be with us than alone so jumped aboard and nestled in Min's lap while I drove the few miles out of town to a new-build bungalow. I parked beside a white van and we both exchanged a knowing look. Could it be this obvious? There were a lot of white vans, and nobody had got a proper look at the one used at the clinic, but this model was certainly dirty like the other one, with mud spattered over the bodywork, obscuring the number plate.

"Do you recognise it?" asked Min.

"It's a white van. Everyone has them. If they had something to hide, they would have cleaned it up before the police came to talk to them. Or, they didn't want to arouse suspicion so left it as it was. Let's go have a chat and see what we think."

Before we got to the door, a powerhouse of a woman came from around the back, rubbing her muddy hands together and whistling. She clearly worked out, her muscles visible because she wore a simple black vest and shorts riding high on her defined thighs.

"Who are you?" she asked, her stance changing.

"I'm Max. I called about what happened yesterday. You said I could come by. This is Min. The dog's called Anxious, but he isn't."

"Ah, right, of course," she nodded, smiling, but her eyes hooded. "I bet the little guy was anxious when you saw him, then you got him home and he was anything but, right?"

"Wow, you're the first person to ever understand that," I gasped.

"My tortoise was Timmy Timid, the only difference being, he truly was," she said, a faraway look in her eyes.

"He was quite rare?"

"Very. Worth more than that stupid parrot," Cindy Cooper grumbled. "That man's hard work. Sorry, I shouldn't be so grumpy. It's been a very trying time. I didn't sleep a wink last night, and the police keep bothering me. Why don't they just get on with finding who did this?"

"Why do they keep bothering you?"

"Said they know my type. Apparently, they think I might have something to do with this. Just because I used to be in the army, they think that means I'm a killer of nurses and vets. It's beyond annoying."

"You were in the army?" asked Min. "But not now?"

"I left a few years back. I still keep in touch with some of them, but I'd had enough. Look, who are you people exactly? What's any of this got to do with you?"

Cindy agreed to talk to us once I'd explained, but she didn't invite us inside. She led us to the back where we sat under the shade of a tree, and she excused herself to wash up after her gardening. When she returned, it was with a glass of water for us and a beer for her—we'd both passed on an afternoon tipple.

Gasping, then wiping her mouth after a long draw on the bottle, she got straight down to business. "I'm a military woman, that's obvious, and yes, if I wanted to do it, I could. And yes, I know about smoke grenades, have quality gear, and certainly have a baseball bat. Not that I would use one. It's better to use a truncheon. They're smaller, harder, and cause more damage."

"You have a truncheon?"

"I do. And a spare baseball bat. Look, the police asked me plenty of questions, but they know the deal. I'm an outsider and have the wherewithal to pull this off, but I absolutely didn't do it. I wasn't involved. Everyone thinks there were at least two people, so it could have been me working from the inside, but no way would I ever hurt anyone like that, and I'd never steal people's animals. I love them too much."

"You have other pets?"

"Sure. And here she comes now." Cindy's whole demeanour softened as an adorable Rough Collie sauntered out of the house, yawning as she sashayed.

Anxious, who until now had been bored, was instantly alert. How he hadn't already smelt her was testament to how tired he was and how much his injury had rattled him. The Lassie lookalike stopped dead in her tracks, looked from Anxious to Cindy, then lay down, her head held high, acting utterly uninterested.

"Make sure you behave," I warned. "No funny business."

Anxious turned, as if affronted, then walked over cautiously and sat in front of his new friend. He held up his paw, playing the sympathy card, and the Collie angled her head away but slowly she turned back and sniffed the offered paw, then licked it once.

Anxious lay down gently next to her, clearly understanding she was an older dog, and they sniffed each other and groaned happily.

"I think it's love," noted Min.

"She's getting on, but she still likes to play," said Cindy. "You watch. Once she's finished showing off she'll be tearing around the garden. Lady's a real lady, but she also likes to go wild if she takes to someone."

Anxious was already up, front legs bent, bum sticking up in the air, yipping at Lady. She sighed, but then she clearly thought better of the coy act and bounded to her feet and raced around the large lawn, barking loudly for Anxious to come and play.

"There'll be no stopping him now. He loves making friends," I laughed.

"Lady's the same," said Cindy.

"Why do you think this happened?" I asked. "Any insights? And given your background, do you think this was someone from the military?"

"As to why, I have no idea. Apparently, there was a lot of ill will between the two veterinary practices, but I didn't know anything about that. I've been here a few years, wanting somewhere quiet, but I'm English and still seen as an outsider by some. I like it, but it gets trying at times."

"Everyone seems friendly enough."

"Sure, they are, but it's always the same in a small town. I've lived in so many places I can't even count them all, and this is no different. I don't know everyone well enough to speculate about the motive, but one thing I can tell you is I doubt this was a military group."

"What makes you say that?" asked Min.

"Because it was so dumb! Who steals animals from a vets? Who kills a nurse and bashes receptionists? It was a major risk. They could have been bitten, seen, or caught leaving. Too many variables. Not a sensible operating style at all."

"We appreciate the insight. One more thing?" I asked. "What's with the van? What do you do for a living, if you do work?"

"I'm a gardener. When I'm not working on my own land, I'm working for other people. I love being outside, and this is the best way to ensure I get to spend as much time as possible with the things I love the most. Animals and nature."

"And were the locals alright with you moving here and setting up business?"

"I got a few choice words from a few, but most were happy to have me. I do a lot of private gardens, and once they've employed me they never fire me. I studied to become a professional gardener after I left the army, so I know what I'm doing. It keeps me fit too."

"Sorry to ask so many questions," I said. "We're just trying to get the full picture. I hope you aren't offended."

"It takes more than this to offend me. I like you both, and I get why you're asking me, but I'm afraid this is a dead end for you guys. I hope you figure it out, though, and please get my tortoise back."

"Was it expensive? And what's wrong with it?"

"They're worth a fortune, but I got it when I was a kid and they were cheap then. Mum and Dad bought him as a birthday present. They had a friend who bred them, no easy thing, and I got him when he was tiny. They kept him when I joined the army, but after that I brought him with me. Collectors would be falling over themselves to have him. You can count on that."

As the barking rose in pitch, we turned to watch the two dogs running laps around the garden. Leaping, spinning, cajoling the other to give chase. Anxious darted under Lady, then spun sharply and headed back the same way before coming up in front of her and rolling over repeatedly, beside himself with joy. Lady leaped high and spun, mid-air, then raced off with him tearing after her.

We sat and watched for a while, the conversation turning to other things, but Lady soon tired and came over to Cindy with Anxious right on her heels. When she lay down, Anxious did the gentlemanly thing and stopped pestering her. He settled beside her, and she scooted over until they were nestled close, having formed a true bond.

"They'll be getting married soon," noted Cindy with a cheery smile.

"I think you might be right," said Min. "Sorry to hold you up. I'm sure you're busy, so we better get going."

"It was no problem. Actually, it was nice to have a chat. You're good people, I can tell, so thank you for not judging."

"Why would we judge?" asked Min.

"Because that's what people do, right? We all do. We look at someone, or speak to them for a few seconds, and we think we know the kind of person they are. We don't. But it's how we're wired. You both let this play out a little before deciding anything. That's good."

We said our farewells, although Anxious wanted to stay. With a final lick of Lady, he reluctantly went over to Cindy for a fuss because he hadn't had one yet, then deigned to follow us back to the campervan.

Neither of us said much as I drove back into town then parked at Erin's, but once we were out of the van we both asked simultaneously, "Do you think it was her?"

With a laugh, we both agreed it was very unlikely. She was no-nonsense, but honest, and a genuine person as far as we could tell. Anxious liked her, too, so that pretty much put her out of the picture.

"Have you had enough?" I asked. "You've got quite a drive home. Sorry it hasn't been very relaxing."

"It's been fun. You know, in a sad way. I'm relieved Anxious is recovered, and I'm glad you found a nice spot. I'll go later on, but I won't stay for dinner. What are you cooking?"

"I'm not sure yet. Probably something quick. Or maybe something super slow," I laughed. "Something that will let me sit in my chair and do nothing."

"Max, you're always doing something. You might sit, but you'll still think."

"True. I'll make us a cuppa, then we can go and have a fun afternoon. Deal?"

"That sounds perfect. Maybe a little nap first?" asked Min with a cheeky wink.

"Now you're talking my kind of language."

We sat under the sun shelter and chatted quietly while we had our tea, then stretched out our legs and sank low in our chairs. It was a perfect summer's afternoon with birds singing, insects buzzing, and life felt just about perfect. Both of us slept for an hour, waking feeling groggy but refreshed once we'd come around.

Anxious was ready for more fun now, too, so we set off down the hill with a spring in our step.

Chapter 11

Harlech Castle may not have been the largest ruin on the North Wales coast, but it was one of the prettiest, and certainly offered a stunning view. We appeared to have timed it perfectly, arriving a little after three with hours of glorious weather ahead of us. A welcome surprise was the shade of the high castle walls to ensure we didn't get too hot and bothered.

After paying, we strolled across the footbridge from the impressive cafe and information centre that spanned the deep moat, no longer full of water. Min took my hand and smiled, her eyes dancing with joy. I laughed, recalling how much she loved bridges for some strange reason, never afraid of heights even though I always got a peculiar feeling in my belly.

Anxious whined from behind, so we turned to find him only a few steps onto the firm wooden boards, sitting with his paw held aloft and his head cocked to the side.

"We aren't falling for it, you silly boy," giggled Min, shaking her head.

"No way, buddy. If you want a fun afternoon, and maybe some treats," I teased, "then you have to cross. It's perfectly safe as long as you don't look over the edge." The moment the words were out of my mouth, I regretted it. Anxious turned to the side and in a panic spun and raced back to the building.

"Come on, you big softy. We aren't scared, so neither should you be," soothed Min, squatting and holding out her hands. "We'll look after you."

"That's right," I agreed, joining Min. "And look, the other dogs aren't worried. You don't want them to think you can't cross a bridge, do you?" I indicated a couple walking two bored-looking Labradors across; Anxious followed them with wide eyes.

Clearly not keen on being laughed at, he stood, shook out the fear, then tore across the bridge, sailed past us, and clacked his way to the far end, only stopping once he reached the large stone portico. He spun, barked at us to hurry up, so, shaking our heads and laughing we joined our fearless pooch and he got a biscuit for being valiant.

Through the portico, we entered a mini wonderland of well-trodden, tough Welsh grass surrounded on all sides by looming stone walls, the enduring remains of what was at one time a much larger fortress on a hill surrounded by the now receded sea.

Already hot, we followed Anxious into the deep shade afforded by the walls and took a moment to admire the ingenuity of people long departed.

"How did they build these things without modern equipment?" mused Min, shading her eyes as she studied the high walls where people walked carefully along the parapet, nothing but a low railing between them and certain death.

"Beats me. They were smart, that's for sure. I bet they had thousands of people hauling rocks, an incredible amount of horses to pull carts, and I can't even imagine how tough a life it must have been for the poor peasants."

"Maybe it was a better time. Simpler. Do your job, eat, sleep, then repeat all over again. Less to worry about. No technology. No worrying about if your car breaks down or you need a new washing machine."

"Maybe it was. It was certainly a very basic life, but I'm sure it was unbelievably hard. Can you imagine existing without electricity? Think what it must have been like living in a castle. No central heating, the only light from candles or roaring fires. They didn't even have glass back then, so the temperatures would be unbearable. Imagine the wind howling through the halls in the middle of winter."

"I guess they must have used shutters or big tapestries. Something like that anyway."

"I never thought of that. Wow, we don't know much about our history, do we? And it wasn't even that long ago."

"I think I'll stick to smart bulbs and decent wi-fi," giggled Min. "Echo, please make my castle warmer."

We sat and leaned against the cool rock, talking about the past, picturing a life living in a small building and working for the local lord, tending a smallholding, keeping animals, sitting by a fire in the evening, mending clothes before an early night snuggled down under itchy blankets and waiting for daylight. What a life that must have been. Were they happy, or too exhausted and beaten by the struggles of life to even have time to wonder if they were content or not? We would never know.

"It puts our own problems into perspective, right?" I said. "Death was just an everyday thing back then. Not hidden away like it is now. We make everything so clinical, and try to sanitise the nasty bits of life, but it was very different for those before us."

"I'm happy to not deal with any gruesome stuff, thanks very much." Min shuddered and scooted over, so I put my arm around her and she cuddled in close.

"Me too," I sighed, wishing we could stay like this forever.

Anxious began to get antsy from sitting for too long, so with his subtle hints of repeatedly pawing at our legs and whining, we told him we'd go and explore.

We took our time, although in truth there wasn't that much to see. Most exciting were the views our high vantage point afforded, and walking around the outside of the castle with the moat and steep, gut-wrenching drop. We marvelled at how on earth they could build in such an inhospitable location, especially when the sea would have been lapping at the foundations while the builders tried to haul the large stones into place.

"Let's go up the tower and walk along the top of the walls," suggested Min, her cheeks flushed with the thought.

"Are you sure?" I asked warily. "It's very high. Anxious wouldn't like it."

"Stop using him as an excuse," teased Min as she nudged me playfully.

"As if! I'm just thinking of the little guy and his dodgy paw."

Anxious dutifully lifted his "poorly" leg and did his best sad puppy dog eyes. I winked at him.

"He doesn't mind waiting for us, do you?" Min waved a biscuit and Anxious was suddenly recovered. He took his treat and retreated to the shade, then lay down and ignored us completely.

"Traitor," I hissed. Laughing, I said, "Fine, but if I fall you'll have to clean up the mess. Remember, it'll be gooey and nasty."

"We'll be fine. There's a railing."

Steeling myself, jittery for some reason when usually heights didn't bother me, I joined Min who was already heading for the tower that led to the battlements. Why was I so concerned? What was going on? I had what I could only describe as "a feeling" that this wasn't right. Maybe I was concerned for Min? The weirdness of the last few days possibly? Something else? Or was I merely nervous of the height?

Against my better judgement, with butterflies in my stomach and my throat very dry, I ducked under the stone lintel and followed Min into the tower, a series of steep, winding, smooth stone steps leading around and around until moments later we emerged into glorious sunlight. Heat bounced off the walls and the air shimmered as Min stood with her back to the sun like an angel, a halo around her blond hair blowing into her face on a gentle breeze.

"Doesn't it feel wonderful?" she gushed. "It's like being a bird."

"Just don't try to fly," I said, smiling at her playful attitude. "But the air is cooler, although the rocks are baking." I reached out and put my hand to the low stone wall, gasping at how much sun they'd soaked up. I also looked over the railing, and spied Anxious keeled over on his side, sleeping happily while he waited for us to descend.

"Come on, let's walk around," said Min, holding out her hand.

With that being all the incentive I needed to risk life and limb, I hurried forward and together we traversed the short path around part of the castle before we stopped to look out to the vast stretch of sand dunes and the sea beyond.

My nerves settled, inexplicably because of the height and the realisation that there was nothing to be afraid of because this was what life was all about. Fun, family, adventure. But when I turned to Min, she wasn't looking so good, and had a deep frown creasing her forehead.

"What's wrong?"

"I just felt off all of a sudden."

"Like I did earlier. Come on, let's go down."

"Yes, good idea. Hold on to me, please?"

"Sure."

We took it slowly back towards the tower, then paused when an elderly couple in walking gear came marching towards us and let them pass. I checked on Anxious and then something caught my eye.

"I think that's Rhys, Erin's brother," I told Min, pointing at him as he hurried across the grass over to a far wall in deep shade.

"I thought he was a mechanic? Shouldn't he be working?"

"Yeah, but he owns the place, so can come and go as he likes, I guess. Maybe he finished early." I watched as he sank to the ground and fished around in a carrier bag then pulled out a can of something and drank greedily. In just a few seconds, he'd discarded it and pulled out another, then sipped it. Even from our height, it was clear that what I suspected was beer had calmed him as he leaned his head against the wall.

"Bit odd to come here to drink, isn't it?" asked Min.

"Erin said he was a bit of a boozer. But I thought that was in the evenings at the pub. Maybe he has a problem."

"Or he likes to hang out here after a hard day and relax. You said he was a nice guy?"

"He was great with Vee. Fixed her up better than ever, and was really friendly. I haven't seen him much since, but he's a decent bloke."

"Can we go down now?" Min still looked rather green, so I nodded, but just as we were about to enter the tower something else stopped me dead.

"What's he up to?" I whispered as I spied a familiar face keeping to the shadows then ducking behind a wall before peering out and watching Rhys.

"Who?"

"That man there, he's spying on Rhys. I met him at the other vets. He's the gardener. He works for quite a few people and businesses in Harlech. He's called Dai. A bit rough around the edges, but friendly. Another one who didn't have a kind word to say about Leo. Why is he spying?"

"Max, he just looks like he's cooling down. It's boiling. Can we please get down?"

"Yes, sorry. It's very weird though. Look, now he's taking photos."

Min put a hand to the railing and sucked in air, her face covered in a sheen of sweat. "I don't feel so great."

"You don't look it either. Come on, I'll help you down."

We descended carefully, and the moment we were on the ground Min sank to her knees then sprawled out and spread her arms, sighing with relief.

"That got to you, didn't it?" I asked, concerned.

"It did. I don't know why, but it really did. I'm never bothered by heights. I think it's the exercise and stress. It's made me jumpy. Dwelling on death. I thought it would be fun, but all I could picture was you falling. What if you died?" Min sat up and our eyes locked. "Max, I couldn't bear it if something happened to you. You must be careful. You being out here all alone, trying to help these communities, and this new calling of yours, it's very worrying. More. It's terrifying. Don't die!" Min sobbed into her hands while I stood there, shocked.

"Hey, it's okay," I said as I squatted. "I'm tough, and getting tougher. Nothing will happen. I'm being careful and not taking any chances. Don't worry about me. Where has this come from?"

"Max, it hit me the minute you drove off that first day in the VW. I panicked. Actually, I had a full-blown panic attack. I didn't know what was happening. That's why I came with your parents the next day. And I was right to worry. There you were, getting drawn into a murder mystery, and it's got worse."

"You should have said. Min, if you want me to stop, then I will. Do you want that?"

"Yes. No. Oh, I don't know," she wailed, flinging her arms up. "You'd give all this up?" Min raised her head and she saw the truth. That of course I would.

"Yes. I would."

"I don't want you to. I know how much this means to you, and that you really are helping people, even if that's partly because you refuse to let go of something once you get started. Stubborn as always. But it's a great thing that you help solve these crimes. You must be careful."

"I will, and I understand. Come on, I think we've had enough for one day, don't you? This is too much for you. Too much for both of us. Go home, get on with your life, and stop worrying."

"But I don't want to go!" Min whispered.

"You don't?" I asked, confused.

"Of course not. You are so dumb sometimes."

"I know," I sighed. "What do you want then?"

"What I want more than anything in the world is to know what I want. Gosh, I sound like such a fool. I'm so sorry for messing you around like this, but life is just too confusing at the moment. You're right, I should go home and stop upsetting you. I'm just making this harder for both of us. I feel like the worst kind of woman imaginable.

Stringing you along, telling you we aren't getting back together then turning up all the time and warning you to not even look at another woman. It's not fair."

"It's love, and it's complicated," I said, shrugging, not knowing what else to say. "Min, I understand, and let's stop going over old ground. I've accepted things, and I thought you had too."

"I had. Have. But I feel like a cow for not letting you go. Maybe that's best for both of us."

My stomach flipped at the words, and I felt sick to the bottom of my very soul. "If that's what you want, I'll accept it, but it isn't what I want and I don't think it's what you do either. Let's not do this again. You know how I feel, and yes, I will continue living this life, doing what I do, as I get the feeling I'm always going to encounter one mystery or another on my travels, but have no doubt, Min, that I will always love you and always want us to be together. Now, don't ever feel bad for feeling confused. That's my fault and we both know it. Life's complicated, we screw up, but that's in the past and now we move forward. Agreed?"

Min wiped her eyes and smiled. "Agreed."

I gave her a minute to sort herself out, actually pleased to have a little space to recover from what was an emotionally draining conversation. Sometimes I truly despised myself for what I'd put us both through, for the hurt and the utter decimation of our marriage, but I still stood by the words I'd just spoken. It was done; we had to move forward. We simply had to.

Anxious was still sleeping, snoring away without a care in the world, oblivious to the insanity we humans inflicted on ourselves and each other. I wandered around the castle grounds, but Rhys and Dai were long gone. What was going on there? Or had I been mistaken and Dai was simply snapping a few pictures of the castle? But why would he? He'd lived here all his life. Maybe he suspected Rhys. I shook my head and told myself to get a grip. Now I really was getting carried away.

Whoever was doing this wasn't someone I'd met yet. Or was it?

Scratching my head, I went to wake Anxious then returned to Min who had cleaned up her face and smiled sheepishly.

"Sorry about that. Ignore me, I'm just being emotional," she said.

"Emotion is what makes us human, Min. No need to apologise. Leave that to me," I grinned.

Arm in arm, with Anxious bravely crossing the bridge without running too fast, we returned to my own private campsite.

Min stayed for a while, fussing over Anxious and lamenting that she had to leave, while I began preparing dinner.

She left not long after I'd peeled and chopped the onions.

"Stupid onions," I muttered, wiping my eyes as they streamed.

Anxious cocked his head and locked his knowing eyes on me.

"Fine, maybe it isn't the onions."

Chapter 12

To cheer myself up, and to ensure I didn't fall out of the habit, tonight's meal was to be a real feast. I had hoped Min would stay, but she had work and a long drive ahead, so I understood. The day had been an emotional one, and not just because of our complex relationship, but because of the people we'd spoken to and the worrying events that had unfolded. I needed this downtime to mull things over, get myself together, and see what percolated into my head.

Although the hot weather made many one-pot dishes rather a sweaty affair, I needed to eat something comforting and hearty, so tonight's feast was to be a slow-cooked pork, cider, and sage hotpot. Basically, posh meat and potatoes. A staple of the British diet and a firm favourite of mine.

Once the diced pork was browned and the leeks and onion fried off—I'd peeled the onions so was determined to use them even though it wasn't strictly necessary—I added the garlic and cider slowly to deglaze the pot, then left the whole thing to simmer once I'd prepared the potatoes. Having to get inventive because I had no oven, I lit the fire and would use the coals to cover the lid later to brown off the potatoes nicely, but for now I had at least an hour and a half to sit and relax whilst I finished off the remaining bottle of Uncle Jack's Rough as Rocks Traditional Cider. A real mouthful in more ways than one, it almost blew my head off when I took the first sip. The aftertaste was surprisingly mellow, though, and if I ignored the floaters and the strange colour, it was pretty decent.

Settling into my chair, I decided to text Erin and invite her for dinner again. She was a fountain of local knowledge, I enjoyed her company, and it seemed only right that I should include her in my search for the killer or killers as this was more about her than it was about me. Plus, it was my way of paying her back for the offer to stay here.

She replied almost instantly using text speak I hardly understood, but I got the gist of it. She'd be over in an hour or so once work was finished and she'd had the chance to clean up and change. I could only imagine the kind of day she'd had if the chaos of the morning was anything to go by, so she certainly deserved to have her evening meal cooked for her rather than ending up eating something unhealthy. I almost invited Rhys, too, but thought better of it as I knew I'd only end up spoiling the evening by asking about the castle, and the last thing I wanted to do was insult my hosts.

Relaxing by the fire, I formulated a plan for the following day, knowing that the longer this went on, the less chance there was of finding out who did it. I needed to speak to Pip properly, see if there was anything she might say that would help. Her relationship with Patrick, her ex, might be significant, and I wanted to get a proper feel for her anyway. With such a violent side, was it possible she did this to get back at Riley, the dead nurse, for some reason nobody else was aware of? Maybe they'd had a relationship too? It was certainly possible.

Then I'd talk to Patrick, see what he might have to say. It was a long shot, but he'd left Ollie and the others in the lurch and struggling to cope by working for the opposition, so maybe he had a grudge. Or maybe he just wanted to get away from Pip.

And after that I was out of ideas. I would have spoken to everybody I could think of, so would have to ask around and see what came up. Maybe visit a few pet shops or call specialist suppliers of parrots and tortoises and see if anyone had offered the missing pets to them. I was clutching at straws and I knew it. All the while, something kept nagging at me. I was overlooking something; I was sure of it. Like I told Min, there was something lurking in a dark corner of my mind that I couldn't pinpoint but was important somehow.

The smells coming from the pot slowly drew me back to the present, so I checked it was on low enough then sat back down and emptied my mind of everything and enjoyed the peace. Anxious remained fast asleep, tucked under the campervan, having just discovered it offered excellent shade. Secretly, I think he'd grown as attached to it as me and wanted to stay close. There was just something about this old vehicle that went beyond a means of transport and somewhere to sleep. It had become a true part of us in a very short time, and already our old life living in a house with all the associated stress and complications seemed like madness.

I would do anything for Min, including giving this up, but I hoped that when we eventually reunited it would be to live in Vee together. That would be one sweet life indeed!

Having finished transferring the potatoes to the pot now the liquor had reduced enough, but not too much, I turned to find Rhys staring into the fire. He was lost deep in thought and acted like he didn't even know I was there, his shoulders hunched and head bowed, his back to me.

I waited to see how long it would take him to say hello, but he apparently had other ideas and just continued to contemplate the flames. Every so often he swayed, clearly under the influence, and eventually I broke the silence by clearing my throat. When he still didn't react, I settled the lid on the pot, checked my watch, then wandered over, strangely reassured when Anxious crawled out on his belly like a commando on a mission, and joined me, staying right by my side, glancing from me to Rhys repeatedly as if he, too, needed reassurance.

"Rhys, you okay?"

"Huh? Oh, hey there, Max. And hey, Anxious. You two had a good day?"

"Let's just say it's been eventful and leave it at that. We asked around, visited a few people, went to the castle this afternoon," I hinted.

"Oh yeah," he mumbled, turning his head away as if distracted by a sound. But there was nothing apart from us, the crackling fire, and the pot simmering away.

"Yes, late this afternoon. It was fun, if quite scary up on the parapet."

"It's a fantastic spot, and nice and cool in the shade. I go there sometimes to chill out. I was there today. I'm surprised I didn't see you. Did your missus like it? I heard she'd come to visit to check on this guy." Rhys squatted awkwardly beside Anxious and ruffled his head.

Anxious sniffed Rhys' leg then seemed to make his mind up about him and rubbed against his hand for more fuss. If Anxious trusted him, I supposed I should, too, but something wasn't right here.

"She left not long ago, but had a nice day, thanks. It's a crazy steep hill to climb, isn't it? We were shattered because we walked all the way down then back up again."

"I've done it a few times, and sure, it's a killer." Rhys frowned, then added, "Sorry, poor choice of words. Do you mind me coming to check out the fire? It looked nice, so I thought I'd come and say hi."

"No problem. In fact, you can stay for dinner if you want? Erin's coming, but I assumed you'd have plans."

"Yeah, I do, but thanks for the offer, mate. Sorry if I'm distant, but it's been one of those days, you know? Had a few drinks, but I don't think it helps really. Just puts me in a sour mood sometimes, and then I can't stop until I get over the hump and am totally plastered. Then I feel like crap the next day and regret it, but I still repeat it over and over. Max, I'm a mess, actually," he admitted, meeting my eyes for the first time since he'd arrived.

"Life's tough at times. What's the issue?"

"Everything. Nothing. This place. Living in my parents' house. Not having my own pad. Even running the business is tough. There's not really enough work around here. It's why I had to take the money for fixing the camper."

"As was right. I expected to pay. Everyone has to earn a living."

"Apart from you. Sorry, that sounded bitter when it wasn't meant to. I just meant it would be nice to not have to worry about everything."

"Money doesn't stop you worrying. It just means you have more time to get stressed about everything else."

Rhys smiled, his cheeks red from the booze, and said, "I wouldn't mind trying it though. It's everything and nothing, I guess. Just life. And I'm already half-soaked. I had a few cans earlier and now I'm off out for more."

"Stay for dinner instead. Some food to soak up the beer."

"Nah, you're alright, mate. But listen, that's not why I came. I almost forgot, but it's Erin's birthday tomorrow and we're going to surprise her."

"Oh, I didn't know. What's the surprise?"

"I heard that you went to Paintball in the Hills? I know those guys pretty well. I go up there sometimes with my mates and we have a blast. It's a fun thing to do. But Erin absolutely loves paintball and goes more than me."

"Does she? She never said." My mind began to whirl at the information, and I felt dizzy, almost sick. "Erin said she'd had a few goes, but never said it was a real interest of hers."

"Yeah, she loves it. Goes all the time. She used to date one of the guys up there. He's out of the picture now, but still works there. He was a good bloke. Bit of a rough one, into a bit of bother, but nothing serious." Rhys shrugged, then added, "So, the surprise is that we're taking her paintballing. I spoke to everyone at her work and they're up for it. Even Aggie and her bloke. Ollie and Pip are keen, and they sure need a distraction, so how about it to make up the numbers? My treat as a thank you for trying to solve this mess. What do you say?"

"That sounds great, and thanks for the invite. But I'll pay my own way."

"It's already done, Max. I booked it for six tomorrow evening. Got an incredible deal, so no worries. I'm not that hard up. You'll come?"

"I will. It sounds like fun. Everyone could do with a distraction. That's a kind thing to do for your sister."

"Yeah, well, it's no biggie." Rhys rubbed his face, clearly embarrassed, then said hurriedly, "See you tomorrow then. Rock up there about six and we'll shoot the hell out of each other." With a wave, he rushed up the garden. The back door slammed shut and a muffled shout came from inside. Most likely he'd tripped in his less than steady state.

With my head reeling, I slumped into my chair, cursing the cup holder for the first time as my bottle of cider bounced out of the mesh. I snatched it from the air before I lost the contents, then downed the strange brew before sighing.

Erin had never once mentioned that she was a real paintball fan. She'd said it was something she'd participated in a few times, but hadn't been for years, and why not mention the boyfriend? Was she covering for him? Why do that unless she believed he might be involved? Could she be? Was it her and this supposed ex-boyfriend? I forced myself to calm down. Erin was a sweet girl and I trusted her. My ability to read people to some degree made me sure she was innocent, but I'd been wrong before and just because I believed something didn't make it true.

Could she be responsible for all this and had put on an act to throw everyone off? Would she attack Aggie and the others, kill Riley and Leo? No, there was absolutely no way.

So why lie?

I was just transferring the pot to the fire when she arrived. Distracted by the deep, meaty aromas and subtle hints of sage, I nearly dropped the lot when she said a cheery, "Hey!"

"Oh, hey. Give me a moment while I put the coals on the lid. That way, we'll have nice and crispy potatoes in our hotpot."

"Hotpot? Yum! That's my favourite. What meat are you using?" Erin eased over to the fire, the scent of perfume strong and enticing, her hair freshly washed and shining. Her make-up was powerful and dark, with very red lips, and her green and white striped T-shirt made her look every ounce a young punk out for a wild night.

"Diced pork shoulder. It should be super soft. I used this crazy cider I picked up in town, and it's worked wonders. Give it twenty minutes and it should be ready. In fact, I know it will. Take a seat, Erin. I need to talk to you."

"That sounds ominous," she said warily as she sat in a camping chair and leaned forward, her brow creased.

"It kind of is," I admitted. "Normally, I wouldn't be so direct about such a sensitive issue, and I certainly don't want to cause offence, but I need to ask."

"Spit it out, Max. I'm a big girl and can handle it. But you do have me worried. Is this about the murders? Have you found something out?"

"Yes, and no."

"Could you be any more cryptic?" she laughed nervously.

"I can try. Listen, I've heard that you actually love paintball and go regularly. That you used to date a guy who works there. What gives? You know it was important, as that's why we went there, but nobody there acted like they knew you that well, and neither you nor them said you were a regular. You must have known about the smoke grenades already, and you kept information from me. Did you hide it from the police too? That's serious, Erin. You must know that?"

Erin's face contorted in a fascinating and concerning way as her mouth opened and closed, her eye twitched, and a vein at her temple throbbed. Colour rose up her neck as she tangled her fingers through her hair and twisted obsessively.

"I... It isn't what you think. I would never... How did you find out? Are you accusing me?"

"This is why I wanted to talk to you. I like you, and we've been getting on great. Normally, I'd snoop and try to uncover the truth, but I believe we're friends?"

"We are. Of course."

"Then let's not mess about. I want the truth. I think I deserve that. You told me about the detective giving you information regards the smoke grenades. Was that true?"

"Yes, it was. I swear."

"But you knew what they were already?"

"Kinda. Yeah, sure, I knew. But I didn't want to look like a suspect. I've bought them from the paintball place. So has Rhys. We like to play. I should have said, I guess, but this has been too much. You understand, right?"

"I'm not sure I do. Why not be upfront?"

"Because I was worried you wouldn't want to be friends, to hang out, and let me tag along with you. Max, this place is so boring. I'm going out of my mind. When this happened, and I know it's a terrible thing to say, but it was scary and exciting. Something actually happened here. When we spoke and it seemed like we might be able to team up and I could be involved in an actual murder investigation, then two, well, I just kept quiet about the paintball. You get that, don't you?"

"Wow, yes, of course. I'm so sorry to ask, but that's why I didn't try to go behind your back. What about this boyfriend?"

Erin shrugged. "He's a loser. He works up there. We only went on a few dates, so he wasn't really a boyfriend. I said I didn't want to see him again as he wasn't my type, and he was way too into the whole scene. Sorry, I should have said, but I didn't want you to think badly of me." Erin paused to think, then asked, "You spoke to Rhys, didn't you? Nobody else knew I dated that dumbo, Benny, apart from him, so he must have told."

"He did, but he didn't think it made you a suspect. So why would you?"

"Because Benny's dodgy, and I knew you'd go looking into him. I never told the police either. You have to trust me on this, Max. Benny's no killer. Dumb, a bit of a plank, actually, but not a killer. He's just, how do I put this without sounding mean? A bit soft. He's easily led, is always being bossed around by the others, and gets into trouble because he doesn't think before he acts, but he's innocent. I spoke to him, just to check, and he was utterly oblivious to any of it even happening. He lives in his own world."

"You're sure about this?"

"I am. Look, if you want, I'll talk to the detectives, but Benny's just a simple lad and doesn't deserve the grief. You trust me, don't you? Please say you do."

"I do, and I'm sorry. Still friends?" I asked, smiling, the relief palpable now she'd explained.

"Yes, friends. Am I still on the case with you? Can I help?"

"That would be great. Are you working tomorrow?"

"Only for an hour early in the morning to catch up on today. Ollie's had enough and isn't opening. It was just people being nosy, so he'll just do emergencies, but I don't need to stay. I need a break from that place anyway. It's been too much for everyone."

"Then we'll spend the day figuring this out. But for now, let's eat!"

"Great. I'm starving."

With an oven glove, I lifted the lid and we both sighed with pleasure as the crispy top of the hotpot was revealed and the delicious aromas hit our nostrils.

I couldn't dish it up fast enough, and Anxious tucked in as keenly as us.

Chapter 13

"Wow, Max, how do you do it?" sighed Erin as she leaned back and rubbed her belly. "I feel like I've just eaten in a posh restaurant, but I'm sitting on a camping chair in my back garden. It's doing funny things to my head."

"It was just a hotpot," I said, beaming with pride, as there's nothing better than someone complimenting you when you did your best.

"Come on, you know that isn't true," she teased. "You really are an excellent cook, aren't you? I can see why you became a chef. It's the little things that make the difference. You put real effort into it, right? Sorry, I wasn't making fun of your name, but I think your parents knew what they were doing when they chose your name. It fits perfectly."

"Don't you dare say that!" I warned with a grin. "I shall hate them forever for what they did to me. I could have been called Frank, or Bill, or pretty much anything but Max. But thank you for the kind words. I do enjoy cooking a lot."

"And it doesn't bother you having to do it out of the camper, or in your outdoor kitchen? I bet you never cooked this way when you worked in fancy restaurants, did you?"

"It was a bit different," I admitted, wondering if I would ever be able to stand again because my stomach felt so weighty. "Although it's all the rage now to cook on an open flame or coals. People pay through the nose for a genuine experience, and lots of places have open kitchens so you can see your food being cooked."

"But you still have all the fancy equipment, and you won't get soaked or freezing in the winter."

"True. So far, I'm enjoying cooking like this immensely, but we'll see how I feel come the autumn."

"As long as you have your shelter, you should be fine. Damp, cold, but fine," Erin laughed. "But don't you miss that old life of comfort and doing what you love the most?"

"Sometimes," I admitted, surprising myself. "I keep telling myself that I don't miss it at all, but I guess I do. I enjoy the cooking but not the stress, and not the way I become obsessed. I certainly don't miss the shouting. No, as long as I keep my hand in and give the raw ingredients the respect they deserve, then I'm at peace with it. Taking my time over the process has been the best idea I've ever had. One-pot cooking forces you to slow down, to actually be part of things rather than oblivious to what's going on around you."

"Sounds like you've finally found your place in the world." Erin turned wistful as her eyes lost focus. "Wish I felt the same."

"Problems?"

"No, not really. Apart from the murders," she said with a weak smile. "I guess I'm just the same as everyone else. Some days it feels as if there's something missing, you know? Like I'm going through the motions rather than living life. As though there's another way, or something else I should be doing instead of working as a receptionist."

"Don't belittle yourself like that. You do a great job, and an important one. People are sad and stressed when they come to you, and you're the first person they see at the vets. You put them at ease, you're great with the animals, and I can tell that you enjoy it."

"That's the thing. I really do! But I'm still just a receptionist. It isn't very glamorous. Not exactly a high-flyer."

"And would you want to be? You might earn more money, but you'd be stressed, get burned-out like I did, and you'd still always think there was something more. Something different you should be doing. If you enjoy your work, you're luckier than almost everyone else with a job. You shouldn't be so hard on yourself."

"Wow, where did that come from? And you're right. I do love my job, and I do love the animals, and seeing that I've helped people and their pets makes me feel good. Maybe I shouldn't be so pessimistic."

"See, that's the attitude to take. Now, I'm going to have to try and move, although it won't be a pretty sight. You sit tight while I clean up."

"I'll help. Then how about a pint at the pub? We can unwind and maybe chat about what we're going to do next?"

"Sounds like fun. You aren't trying to keep me occupied so I don't stew on Min leaving, are you? I think you're much smarter than you let on sometimes."

Erin winked, then laughed loudly as she said, "You got me! I think I know you well enough to know that you miss her an awful lot. Max, you're a great guy, and she's a lucky woman, but there's no point sitting around thinking about what might happen. You have an important job to do here, and I know you'll solve this."

"How do you know?" I asked, interested in her insight.

"Because now you have me to help!" She burst into a fit of laughter, then groaned as she pushed off from the chair and stood. "I made it! Come on, let's get the dishes done. Um, is Anxious okay? He hasn't moved."

Taking her offered hand, I managed to stand, and we stared down at the bloated pooch who was on his side, eyes glazed, and motionless.

"He's in doggie paradise. Blissed out on hotpot. We need to stop eating so much. We'll be rolling down the hill otherwise."

"Then stop being such a good cook," giggled Erin, then began gathering up the admittedly small amount of washing up.

While she began sorting things out, I emptied the rest of the meal into Tupperware, stowed it in the fridge, then put water in the cast-iron pot so it could bubble away while we cleaned up. Leaving it until last meant the water stayed cleaner in the washing-up bowl, and it was easier to clean.

We worked well as a team, and Erin seemed to instinctively understand my set-up, so we fell into an easy routine like we'd been doing it for years.

My concerns of earlier were forgotten as we chatted and joked around, but I got a strange pang of guilt, as though I was cheating on Min by enjoying another woman's company. I knew it was silly, and that I would never act on anything, but I also knew that if Min was having the same enjoyable evening with another man I would be very jealous. Good or bad, I wasn't sure, but I accepted there was nothing wrong with my feelings and it was perfectly natural.

I freshened up, then it was time to hit the pub. Anxious was reluctant to move, but once standing and realising he could actually walk, he perked right up and was keen to be off. We wandered through the sleepy town, the tourists mostly gone for the day now, although it was still busy at the castle which was now shut, with people sitting on the wall by the moat enjoying their fish and chips suppers, happy and tired with sunburned faces. Children bounced around, playing in the small park or racing along the walls, while parents revelled in a moment of respite from the long day, looking forward to a chilled glass of wine once they got back to their accommodation or one of the numerous local campsites.

Erin led the way to a large field not far away, so Anxious raced around hunting for elusive rabbits and burned off his dinner, his paw now totally healed. Once he'd exhausted himself, we headed to the pub, a very local pub for local people, off the beaten track and not a place the tourists would easily find.

At least, that's what I expected as we turned yet another corner and I lost my bearings, but I was surprised to find that the pub was set on a spacious plot with a large beer garden full of people sitting at picnic benches and tucking into a late dinner or enjoying a drink on the glorious evening.

The sound of mirth and quite a bit of mayhem from inside came as a shock, and I turned to Erin with eyebrows raised.

"Yeah, it gets pretty rowdy. There isn't much to do around here, but one thing we are good at doing is drinking and gossiping. Don't be surprised if people start asking questions."

"What kind of questions?" I eyed up the groups of locals warily as they stared at us and muttered quietly to each other.

"About you, how come a stranger thinks he can solve a double murder, how long it will take you, what you had for breakfast, the colour of your undies? Everything." Erin shrugged as she tugged at my arm and dragged me into the pub.

Feeling rather daunted and apprehensive, the moment we stepped inside I knew my concerns were valid. While outside was for tourists, inside was a much more local affair. The pub was dark, with low ceilings, ancient oak beams, a large inglenook with an open fire burning even though it was one of the hottest days of the year, and the place was half-empty.

All eyes focused on us as we approached the bar, where a smiling Aggie greeted us with a startlingly loud, "HELLO?" that she made a question for some unfathomable reason.

Several locals groaned, seemingly still not used to her bellowing.

"Aggie, what are you doing here?" I asked, unable to hide my surprise.

"I'm the barmaid. I work here a few nights just to get out of the house. And my Kent likes a drink, so this way I can keep an eye on him," she said, checking nobody was eavesdropping as she leaned forward, forgetting that she was speaking so loudly they could hear her in the next village.

"Aggie likes to keep busy," said Erin, beaming at my confusion.

"Right, of course."

"Did you catch the murderer yet?" she asked.

"Not yet, no, but you'll be one of the first to know if I do."

"Good lad. Now what'll it be, Max? The usual for you, Erin? And you better watch that brother of yours. He's been knocking them back like a Whippet without his dinner."

"Like a Whippet?" I asked, not understanding.

"Yes. Fast and furious," laughed Aggie, amused by her joke, if that's what it was.

"He's been drinking more lately," sighed Erin. "There's nothing I can do about it. I don't think he's too happy."

"Sometimes people get into a slump," I said, not wanting to betray a confidence and divulge things we'd spoken about.

After we were served, we turned to survey the room, and I wasn't in the least surprised to find the customers were still watching us. Anxious growled, warning them to mind their own business, but his heart wasn't in it and nobody seemed to take the hint anyway.

An old man wearing a chequered farmer's shirt, purple corduroys, and a bow tie marched over, his cane tapping at the flagstones, his posture that of a man who'd spent a lifetime in the army. He stopped in front of us, ran a hand through Brylcreemed silver hair, and declared, "You're that fellow."

"I am?"

"Yes, the one who's going to save the day, apparently. Let me tell you one thing, young whippersnapper. We don't take kindly to people interfering in our business around these parts. Don't you go waltzing in here upsetting the apple cart and... and, er, tipping the apples everywhere. Nobody wants to be stomping on manky apples!" He frowned as he thought over his words, puffed out his pigeon chest, then waved a crooked hand at me and added, "Or there will be hell to pay."

"I'm not sure I understand what you're saying," I admitted. "But I'll be sure to think on it."

"You do that," he grunted. "Erin." He nodded, then said, "Call me Major. Everyone does."

"Max." We shook hands, his grip firm. "Is there anything you can tell us about the incidents, Major?" I asked. "Anything you think might help? Have you spoken to many people about the deaths?"

"Is he all there?" the Major asked Erin with a frown. "Are you all there, son? You seem wishy washy. Away with the fairies kind of fellow, are you? One of those hippies with your long hair and your big beard. We all know what you lot get up to. Sitting around smoking wacky backy in the nude and listening to Jimi Hendrix. You a joss stick snorter? I bet you are. Playing with crystals and fondling ferns. Is that you, Max? Are you a freaky fern fondler? You one of those, eh? Are you?"

"What if I am?" I asked, feeling defensive and bewildered by his forthright attitude.

"No need to be rude, Major," soothed Erin, stifling a laugh as her eyes streamed with mirth. "Max is trying to help, so you should be happy about that. It's been a terrible time for everyone, and he could have just left us to it. But he's staying on to see if he can uncover the truth. Don't be so rude."

"I wasn't being rude, young missy," he huffed, standing straighter and waving his cane at us.

Anxious barked a warning, but the Major ignored him.

"You sounded rude to me," said Erin. "I haven't seen Max fondle a single fern, although I did see him stroke a hydrangea," she whispered, creasing up as she wiped her eyes.

"Nonsense! How do we know it wasn't him? Was it you, lad? Is that it, eh? You come here and start murdering the poor locals and molesting our shrubbery? Got a thing for the Welsh, do you?"

"I love the Welsh!" I protested. "And you aren't Welsh, are you? No accent."

The entire room fell silent as a chill ran down my spine. The Major turned beetroot and gasped. With shaking hands, he jabbed me in the chest and hissed, "What did you just say? I'll have you know I am as Welsh as a leek, and as devout a Welshman as Tom Jones."

"He lives in America, doesn't he?" I asked.

"Don't you dare start accusing Tom Jones of being foreign. He doesn't live there, he just visits. He's the greatest singer this country ever produced and makes the best music this side of Liverpool."

"What about the Stereophonics?" asked Erin.

"Now you're just making words up," huffed the Major. "Go on, I dare you to say a bad word about our dear Tom. National treasure he is. I'll tan your hide if you do."

"I didn't say anything bad about him," I insisted, now thoroughly confused by the way the conversation was heading. "Look, can we start again? I'm just trying to help Erin and Ollie and the others find the killer. But I'm not the police, just a traveller trying to do what I can. Anything you could do to help would be appreciated by everyone."

"Then why didn't you just say so?" he asked, smiling warmly and patting me on the back.

I spun to Erin, eyebrows raised, but she just giggled and said, "The Major likes to get the measure of people when he first meets them, Max. Don't you, Major?"

"I might be rather abrupt with strangers, but I was just checking you out, lad," he said with a wink.

"Um, right. Okay," I said warily.

"Mine's a pint of Best," said the Major with a nod to Aggie who, like everyone else, had been listening to every word.

"Let me get that," I said, knowing I was expected to pay anyway. I paid for the drink, then followed the Major over to a table in the corner, catching Erin's eye. She smiled, clearly enjoying herself immensely.

Once seated, the Major wasted no time getting down to business.

"People have been talking, and there's only one obvious answer. I spoke to those detectives and told them everything, but they don't seem that interested in us or our problems. It's down to us to solve this, and I think you can lend a hand, Max."

Erin stifled a giggle as I waited for the Major to continue, but I was clearly meant to say something, so said, "Thank you. That's very kind."

With a grunt and a nod, the Major said, "I don't like to speak ill of the dead, but Leo was a bad sort and it doesn't surprise me he was killed. But poor Riley was a kindhearted fellow and didn't deserve to die like that. Now, as to who did it, it's obvious to anyone with half a brain."

"It is? Who was it then?" I asked.

"This pains me to say so, but have you spoken to Cindy Cooper, the tortoise owner?"

"Yes, earlier today. She seems nice. Very friendly once you get to know her."

"She's an outsider and she's trouble," hissed the Major, straightening his already straight bow tie.

"Come on, Major. That's unfair. She's lived here for years and is lovely," sighed Erin. "Let's not go over this again."

"She's a woman! She calls herself a soldier, but she's a female woman. Trouble is what that lass is, I tell you."

"It wasn't her," I said. "And if I didn't know better, I could say you're being rather sexist there, Major."

"Me? As if! I've got no issue with women being in the army, as long as they don't get given guns," he huffed. "But I do have an issue with them beating up dead nurses."

"What's this?" I asked Erin.

"It was ages ago. Cindy floored Riley. He said something disparaging and she just punched him. Knocked him out cold. She never spoke to him again."

"And you never said?"

"I didn't want to taint your opinion as I knew you'd speak to her. I like her. I think she's great, actually, but some around here won't let sleeping dogs lie."

"She had the motive, and the strength to carry out the crime," insisted the Major. "She's built like a brick outhouse and could easily have killed Riley and Leo. Ask anyone. You've seen all those muscles, and she has a terrible attitude."

"Because she won't take any nonsense from you," said Erin, shaking her head.

"I deserve respect, but she's rude."

"But why would she do it?" I asked. "And she had her tortoise stolen."

"That's just a ruse. She's smart, but not smart enough to fool me." The Major tapped his cane against the floor and gripped it tightly. "She had the motive because she hated Riley for whatever reason. Nobody knows why."

"Then what's the motive for killing Leo and taking the animals, even if she did have a problem with Riley?" I asked, intrigued.

"It's obvious. She hated them both and this was the perfect cover. Act like it's someone who has it in for vets and wants to sell animals, when really it's just a grudge because they both wronged her." With a nod, the Major stood, downed his pint in a few gulps, then turned and left.

"That was..."

"Odd?" laughed Erin. "Ignore him. He's old-fashioned and has never taken to Cindy because she refuses to pander to him. Cindy is a no-nonsense woman who knows her own mind, and someone I like very much. But she rubs some folk up the wrong way, especially the Major."

"So you don't think it could be her?"

"Absolutely not."

"Then who could it be? We're running out of suspects, Erin."

"Let's just enjoy the rest of the evening and tomorrow we'll go and visit Pip and Patrick. How does that sound?"

"You have a deal," I agreed hurriedly, looking forward to a quiet evening without murder on the menu or any more trouble.

Then the door slammed open and Rhys staggered in.

Chapter 14

"Get me another pint, Aggie," slurred Rhys, his colour up, shirt buttoned wrong, and dirty jeans hanging so low I worried for his decency.

Truth be told, he'd lost all his decency already and looked absolutely awful. Drinking may be fun for some, and certainly in moderate doses, but he was not a happy drunk and it clearly wasn't doing anything to help his mental state.

"No more for you, Rhys Collins," barked Aggie, for once shouting on purpose.

"You what!?" he spluttered, hanging off the doorframe then releasing it and stumbling into the pub. "You're cutting me off?"

"I am. Now go home and sleep it off. You've had enough."

"Fine. Suit yourself. I'll pull my own pint." Rhys made a lunge for the brass rail around the bar but missed. He somehow managed to grab hold of a stool, but his momentum was too great and he crashed over, clutching the stool like he was trying to save its life.

"Does he get like this much?" I asked Erin as we went to his aid.

"Sometimes. He finds life difficult and resorts to the beer. His mates should know better, but they aren't real friends, just drinking buddies. I bet they're out there laughing about the state he's in, although they're probably as messed up."

"Let's get him home."

Rhys was almost unconscious, but we managed to get him standing then perched on the stool with us holding on to him. Aggie sloshed a coffee onto the bar, scowling, then turned to serve a customer.

"Drink this," I ordered, and held the mug up.

"Ish it beers?" he slurred. "I fancies a pint, I does. Lovely stush." Rhys garbled a few more words but they were incomprehensible, so I put the mug to his lips and he drank, unaware of what he was doing.

"He should be ashamed," sighed Erin, wiping her eyes.

"Don't be too hard on him."

"Why not? You don't see me getting into this state. It's gross and embarrassing. Everyone will know."

"So what if they do?" I asked, surprised she cared what others thought. "If they're nice people, they'll understand he's going through a hard time. And if they don't, then why bother with what they think?"

"Max, I'm not dumb. I understand that, but this is a small place and the gossip gets extreme. I don't need the extra hassle."

Once Rhys had finished his coffee, he sobered up enough to stand with a little help. He mumbled an apology to Aggie, who was now more concerned than angry, and she wished him well as we left our drinks half-finished and took Rhys outside.

The cooler air after the stifling pub seemed to work wonders, and Rhys was quite steady on his feet as we walked past the picnic benches, the one with his mates erupting into cheers as Rhys saluted.

"What a bunch of losers. They should know better than to encourage him," snarled Erin as she gave them the finger. They jeered, then returned to their drinking as we left the beer garden.

We weaved our way back to the house, Rhys sobering up rapidly because of the climb and the coffee kicking in. Halfway back, we paused for him to catch his breath and to give us a break from his considerable weight, and sat on the wall outside the castle.

"I'm sorry," mumbled Rhys, his head down, the smell of booze still strong, as though he was sweating pure beer. "I know I should stop. It's pathetic. I'm going to, you wait and see."

"Don't make promises you can't keep," snarled Erin, jumping up in a rage, startling Anxious who leaped onto the wall to avoid her wrath.

"I'm not. I'm done. I'm getting myself mixed up in all kinds of trouble because of the drinking. I should stay home rather than doing what others pay..."

"Others pay what?" I asked, not liking where this was heading.

Erin and I exchanged a look as Rhys coughed.

"Nothing. Doesn't matter."

"Rhys, have you done something?" asked Erin softly. "If you have, then you can tell us. We'll help. If you're involved in something, you have to tell us. It's important."

"No, it's nothing, I swear. I'm just drunk and rambling. Can't even remember what I was saying now."

Anxious barked, then sniffed at Rhys' shirt before sitting and whining.

"Yes, I don't believe him either," I told Anxious. "Rhys, are you involved in what's been happening around here? You need to admit it if you are. What's going on?"

"I had nothing to do with any of it," he shouted, heaving off the wall and clearly about to make a run for it.

Erin grabbed his shirt and yanked him back until he sat with a grunt and hung his head.

"What did you do?" demanded Erin. "Tell me you didn't murder anyone? Tell me, Rhys. Tell me!" She shook him so hard I heard his teeth rattle and I feared Erin was about to throw him into the dry moat. It might not be full of water, but it was still dangerous, and he was in no fit state to climb back out.

"No way! I'd never hurt anyone, you know that. How could you even think such a thing?" Rhys stood and spun, suddenly sober. "I would never steal animals or clobber everyone. Especially you. I know I get crazy sometimes, but hurt people? Shame on you."

"Then what did you mean?" asked Erin, not backing down. "What were you paid to do? How are you involved?"

"I'm not involved. I told you, that's not me."

"Let's just cool it," I said as calmly as I could, even though inside my blood was boiling and I felt so close to being able to put the pieces together. "Rhys, tell us what you were going to say. What have you got drawn into? Nobody will judge you, but—"

"I will," growled Erin.

I shot her a warning look as I continued, "—you should tell us. You'll feel better if you do."

"Maybe." Rhys slid off the wall onto the pavement, then shuffled around to face us.

Anxious took an opportunity and clambered down my outstretched legs, then lay beside Rhys, head on his lap. Rhys played with his ears absentmindedly as he took a deep breath.

"I just started hanging with the guys too much. You know what they're like. A little bit dodgy. Business hasn't been too great, so I started doing up some vehicles they brought in. Only two, and I'm not even sure they were nicked, but I didn't ask too many questions either."

"Oh, Rhys, you silly sod." Erin hopped from the wall and sat beside her brother, then cradled his head in her lap as he slumped sideways and began to sob quietly.

I said nothing. They were there for each other, and it wasn't my business. If Rhys was repairing stolen vehicles, then he should have known better, and clearly he did. He was a mess because of the guilt, and it seemed obvious he regretted his involvement. I wasn't about to report him, but wondered if that was right or wrong on my part. He was just a man trying to make his way in the world and had taken a wrong turn, but I was in no position to judge. If this was the last of it, and I guessed it was, then didn't he deserve a second chance?

Rhys dried his eyes a few minutes later, clearly embarrassed by his show of emotions. He avoided eye contact, but then clearly made a decision and turned and focused on me.

"Sorry about that. I'm not normally a crier, but it's got too much for me. I knew I shouldn't have done it, but I was getting desperate. That's no excuse, and it was wrong. I told the guys I wanted nothing more to do with it, and I think they freaked themselves out by getting involved with suspicious characters anyway. So, it's done. No more dodgy work at my garage. I promise. And I truly do mean that. Will you tell? Am I going to go to prison?"

"I don't think you go to prison for things like that," I said, utterly unsure of what the punishment would be. "But I won't tell as long as you keep your promise. Can I trust you, Rhys? Are you a good guy?"

"He's one of the best, Max," said Erin, putting her arm around her brother. "You should have told me. I could have helped."

"Do you know how embarrassing that would have been?" said Rhys. "I'm your big brother. I'm meant to look out for you, not the other way around. It's shameful."

"There's no shame in admitting when things go wrong or you screwed up," I told him. "Trust me, I speak from bitter experience. I blew up my whole life and am trying my best to put things back together, but you're on the right track by realising what you did was wrong and stopping it. Don't be too hard on yourself."

"Max is right. But I get it. Maybe you need to start specialising," suggested Erin. "Do what you always said you wanted to do and be the go-to guy in Wales for restoring campervans and fixing them up. You're so good at it and have a real knack, plus you know just about everything about VWs. You need to start advertising and getting some high-paying customers like Max."

"That's right," I agreed. "You could make a fortune."

"That's what I've already started doing. It's building up slowly, but I got greedy and wanted more cash for advertising. It's expensive. But I'm getting there, and have a massive fit-out booked for next week, and one a month after, so things are looking up and I'm going to see good money from it."

"So, why are you so depressed?" asked Erin.

"The usual. I'm living in my parents house with my little sister, I have no real friends, and of course the big one. Nobody to share my life with."

"You want a girlfriend?" asked Erin.

"Of course I do! Who doesn't want someone to talk to at the end of the day? To cuddle up to. And, er, you know."

"What's your type?" I asked, suddenly feeling inspired, convinced I had the perfect woman in mind for him.

"Someone who's no-nonsense, pretty, but not in too girly a way. They have to be fit, and like the outdoors, and they must love animals."

"But you guys don't have any animals, do you?"

"Not at the moment, but I really want to get another dog. Our family dog passed a few years ago and it feels empty without her. It's time to have another dog to share our life with."

"I'm sure the right person will come along," I said. "Maybe sooner than you think."

Erin and Rhys stared at me until I began to feel uncomfortable, and I checked my hair in case there was something stuck there.

"You daft lump," laughed Erin.

"What? Why are you both staring at me?"

"Max, you might be a smart guy, but you'd make a terrible poker player," said Rhys. "You're grinning like an idiot. It's obvious you think you can fix me up with someone. But please, the last thing I need is a matchmaker. I'm not about to go on a blind date or anything like that. Forget I said anything, and do not," he warned, "try to get me together with someone. You've only been here five minutes, so don't even know anyone."

"I wouldn't dream of it. Come on, I think it's time to go home, don't you?"

"Sorry you didn't get to enjoy your drinks," mumbled Rhys. "And sorry for the blubbering. I don't normally break down like this."

"Hey, we're friends. It's not a problem."

"And we, my daft big brother," said Erin as she hugged Rhys, "are more than friends. We're family. Don't you ever forget it."

Anxious skipped off ahead as we made our way rather slowly back to the house. Rhys was still slightly unsteady on his feet, and I expected he'd have a raging hangover in the morning, but maybe this was the wake-up call he needed to finally get his act together.

I said goodnight to them both at the bottom gate, and Rhys apologised once more before going ahead while Erin lingered for a moment.

"Sorry about that. Not the night I had in mind, but maybe we got something out of it after all."

"Maybe. That Major fellow was an oddball. Is he always like that?"

"Yeah, always. He's one of the local characters, and before you get any ideas, don't go suspecting Cindy. The Major was just gossiping and he holds a grudge."

"I'm sure you're right. Think Rhys will be okay?"

"He'll be fine. Max, I understand if you want to report him. He's done a bad thing, so maybe he deserves to be punished."

"It's not my business. And like he said, it might not even have been anything illegal. He just didn't ask."

"Come on, don't play dumb." Erin put her hands on her hips and held my gaze, her intense stare quite unnerving.

"Fine," I laughed, hands held up, "he's got involved with a bad group and let them talk him into something when he knew better. But he won't do it again. If he wants to hand himself in, that's his business, not mine."

"I don't know if he'll do that," admitted Erin. "Now I'm in a quandary. Should I tell on my brother for doing something that's most likely illegal? What should I do?"

"It's not for me to say. It's a tough world out here, Erin, and sometimes we have to make difficult decisions. You do what you think is right, the same as I'm sure Rhys will."

"Goodnight, Max. Sleep well. And sorry again about this."

"See you in the morning. Are you still coming with me?"

"Sure, if you want me to?" she asked, brightening.

"Of course. Come get me after work?"

"Absolutely."

Erin turned to leave, but Anxious had other ideas and rubbed against her leg. She laughed as she gave him a huge fuss until he was satisfied, then waved over her shoulder as she headed wearily for the house.

"Sometimes it's easy to forget how lucky we have it, Anxious," I told him.

Anxious cocked his head and barked in agreement, then fixed his eyes on my pocket.

"You're hungry again?" I asked, shaking my head.

A piercing yip was all the answer I needed, so I broke a biscuit in half and he took it gently then crawled under Vee to eat in his new den.

Settling into the chair with a cider, I sipped it slowly as I mulled over the peculiar evening and the revelations that had surfaced. It wasn't so much what had been said that got me to thinking, as what hadn't. I also had other plans I wanted to put into action, but that would have to wait for the morning.

Tomorrow would be an interesting day, of that I was certain. Rhys was a smart man, and I knew he'd do the right thing. But what if I was wrong? What if this had been his way of admitting he played a part in the murders? Maybe not the killer, but possibly the accomplice? Was he covering for one of his mates? Someone he'd got into trouble with and owed a favour? Money debts to an unscrupulous loan shark? All of it was possible, yet it wasn't very convincing. The state he'd been in, he would have most likely confessed to anything.

The paintball sounded like fun, and I was actually looking forward to the chance to blow off some steam and see what all the fuss was about. I'd have to nip out early and get Erin a birthday card as I hadn't had the chance this evening.

Something Rhys had said hit home as I sat and considered the day's events. It really was at times like this that I wanted Min here to talk things over with. Not just a sounding board, but company. Someone who I could sit in silence with and it not feel weird. Quite the opposite. It made me feel more like me than at any other time. Just the sounds of someone else nearby, even when they weren't in the same room.

Tomorrow I would talk with Pip and her ex, Patrick, and see if I could get to the bottom of this. And maybe by then the missing pieces would present themselves. They were already there, I knew they were, but for the life of me I couldn't pinpoint what I was overlooking.

Suddenly I jumped up, almost upending my cider, and decided cup holders in chairs simply weren't worth the trouble. I put my bottle on the small, fold-up table instead, then went to make up the bed before it got too dark. Once it was done, I felt a lot better about things, so settled back down after putting a few small pieces of kindling on the fire, more for the noise of the dry wood crackling than anything else.

I must have dozed off because when I woke up, startled by I didn't know what, I saw a bat fast approaching my face and managed to whip my head aside just as it made contact.

I saw stars and almost blacked out, but kicked out with my foot. The pain lanced up my big toe and right up into my groin, but there was a winded *oomph* from my attacker as I leaped up with Anxious suddenly alert and barking loudly as someone ran off.

We gave chase, but they leaped the gate and were gone into the night. By the time we were through, there was no sign of them, and with no streetlights it was pitch black away from the dying embers of the fire. I checked my watch. Three in the morning. Whoever it was had waited until they knew I'd be fast asleep and probably couldn't believe their luck when they found me in the chair.

Rubbing at my ear where the bat had caught me a glancing blow, I went back to the van, stoked the fire, and waited, ears primed for any sound.

Anxious remained by my side, wide awake, until dawn broke an hour later and the birds greeted a new day. It felt more like the last day on earth than another picture-perfect day in paradise, and I wondered whether the killer was sleeping soundly or formulating a plan to finish me off and stop me snooping once and for all. Was it a warning, or had they intended to kill me too?

This was suddenly becoming way too personal.

Chapter 15

I was sipping coffee by five, but held off on calling the police until seven. I left a message for the detectives in charge and received a call back ten minutes later. After explaining what had happened, we chatted a little about the case, but there were no new leads and little they could tell me. I explained everything I had been doing, not that it had been much since we'd last spoken apart from asking around and chatting with the pet owners, and was told to be careful and to file a report at the station.

With little else to do so early apart from mope, I did exactly that, and managed to catch up with one of the detectives while I was there. He looked tired and not that interested in me or anything much else, but it was early, he'd already been working for an hour, and the murders weren't the only thing he had to deal with.

On the way out, I bumped into Rhys.

"Wow, you look a lot better than I thought you would," I beamed, admiring his smart black shirt, clean jeans, freshly washed hair, the mix of aftershave and shampoo a much more pleasing smell than the beer of yesterday.

"And I feel it too. Max, thank you for last night. It's a bit hazy, but your words hit home and I'm sticking to my promise. No more boozing, no more moping around, and no more secrets. I won't give the police any names, but I'm going to admit what I did and take the consequences. I don't know what that will be, but I have to clear my conscience. I'm not a criminal, and I refuse to go through life regretting my actions, so I'm going to own up. Thank you." Rhys slapped me on the back, then decided it wasn't enough and pulled me into a tight bear hug.

"Hey, it's not down to me. I told you it was your decision, and you should do what you thought was right. I'm glad you're here though. Just be honest, and I'm sure you'll be fine."

"Let's hope so. Wish me luck?"

"Good luck. And Rhys?"

"Yeah?"

"We still on for tonight? Paintball at six?"

"If they don't lock me up, you can count on it." He smiled weakly, patted Anxious, then marched towards the station.

A cloud of indecision fogged my mind, but then I figured I should warn him so called Rhys back and explained what had happened in the night. He was concerned and angry, and said to be careful. I told him to watch out for anyone suspicious too. With a knowing nod, he squared his shoulders and went to salve his conscience.

After buying a card for Erin, I was back home by eight and feeling peculiar. This was the first time since I'd hit the road that I felt my life was in danger. Someone was out to either warn me off or stop me dead in my tracks, and neither sat well with my sense of justice. Self-preservation, on the other hand, was important for obvious reasons, making me question my entire approach to vanlife and the communities I encountered.

Was I being stupid? Was it worth the risk? What if Min had been here? No, I was determined to see this through. If the police still had no leads, then I had to do whatever I could to uncover the truth. I owed it to Erin, Ollie, even Aggie, to solve this. I'd never forgive myself if something happened to any of them. Even Rhys deserved some help, and meeting him at the station confirmed my opinion of him—he was a good guy and would battle his way through the demons currently haunting him.

He turned up half an hour later looking like the cat that got the cream. I was surprised to see him so soon, but he hurriedly explained that he'd spoken to an officer, admitted that he'd done work on vehicles that he thought might have been stolen, and not filed any paperwork. They pressed him for names, but when he point-blank refused to give anyone up they lost interest and said that they would be in touch.

"And that's it?" I asked, amazed.

"No. That's what I said and the guy just laughed. He said I'd be called back in when they had time as they were mad busy, and I'd need a lawyer, which they would appoint. I'm most likely looking at a fine or some community service, but the officer reckoned I won't be shut down or anything like that, and without giving any names there isn't much of a case. I might not have to do anything. Without a trail, there's nothing they can do. I feel bad for the people who lost their cars, if they were stolen, but all I've done is repair cars without the proper documentation. My guts are still churning, but I'm relieved I owned up."

"That's great, Rhys. I'm proud of you. Well done!"

"Thanks, Max, and now I'll definitely see you later. Be careful today. If someone attacked you, be sure to watch your back."

"I will. Don't worry about me."

With a nod, Rhys left with a spring in his step.

I needed to stay busy, and there were things to be done anyway, so I fed Anxious as he was doing that thing where he sat and stared at me, then his bowl, like he despaired of the fact it didn't auto-fill if I was slow to feed him.

"Sorry about that. I'm a bit distracted today," I chuckled. "But you did a great job warning off the bad man last night, so thank you."

Anxious wagged, sweeping his tail cross the bare patch of grass he'd worn beside his bowl, then jumped to his feet as I gave him a healthy scoop of dried food, much to his disdain.

"Hey, that's more than enough. You're supposed to have less than that, but we have a busy day ahead, then paintball this evening. Do you want to play paintball?"

A garbled bark through a mouthful of food was my reply, so I left him to it while I arranged things in the kitchen then moved on to the van. I hauled the grey water waste up to the house and disposed of it in the correct drain, then returned and filled up the tank for the sink with clean water and topped up my water bottles too. The sink and hob, along with counters, had a good scrub, then I set to work on the rest of the interior. Wiping, polishing, and spraying with wood cleaner until everything gleamed.

It was important to stay on top of things and give Vee the love she deserved. Rather than treating it like a vehicle, I wanted to care for my home like I would any other. I even cleaned underneath the Rock-n-Roll bed and got rid of the fluff and dog hairs using the small, handheld vacuum that did a surprisingly thorough job.

With the compact solar system checked over and everything working flawlessly, I turned my attention to the series of small cupboards. The built-in storage in a classic VW was limited to say the least, but the design was excellent and with all the original fixtures and fittings, I owed it to the history of the vehicle to ensure it remained pristine.

Opening the tiny doors allowed for some limited ventilation, but I decided to re-arrange my meagre belongings to better allow for airflow and ensure no nasty mould or funky smells built up. There wasn't much I could do about the shoe storage apart from give everything a good spray, but inside the main section of the van I went to town maximising space and folding clothes, bedding, and towels as compactly as possible. Come the cooler weather, I'd be wanting the room, so it paid to plan ahead to see what I could realistically expect to carry around with me.

One particular cupboard had always given me trouble. A tiny, vertical space where the hinges creaked and a board rattled on the side. I hauled out my toolbox and fixed the hinge, then knelt on the bench seat to tackle the wonky panel.

Made of thin, dark ply, the board itself seemed fine, but it had come away because the panel pins had worked themselves loose. Rather than just tap them back in, I couldn't resist a behind-the-scenes peek at how things were constructed, thinking if I removed the wood I could then straighten the nails before re-using. With a flathead screwdriver, I prized the panel free enough to grip it carefully in one hand, then slid the screwdriver down until the whole section popped out, sending me sprawling back onto the seat with the prized section held aloft, thankfully undamaged.

Placing the board aside carefully on the counter, I scooted forward and peered into the inner depths of the van. With my phone as a torch, I studied the framework the other side of the cupboard, visible as it was a small dividing wall.

"What was I thinking? It's not the wall of the van, it's just the back of the ply," I muttered, wondering what had got into me. I was tempted to remove the back panel, as that would show me the skin of the metal, but what was the point? I was desperate for something to do, that was it. Biding my time until Erin arrived.

"Still, while I'm here I can see if this really is original," I said to nobody. I let the light linger on the faded printing on the back of the board, but it was just numbers and code for the ply. Just as I was about to fetch the panel and replace it, light glinted off something behind the central stud.

"A certificate from the person who kitted out the van?" I wondered, then teased out the fragile slip of paper and sat to read it.

Scrawled on an oblong of yellowing, thick but brittle paper in scratchy capital letters, were the words: HELP ME.

I turned it over; the back was blank.

My heart beat fast, but then I shook my head at the ingenuity of a man almost five decades ago who had mostly likely been laughing with his co-workers as he wrote a note, tucked it behind the stud, then tapped the panel into place. Maybe it was a joke they all took part in? Something to brighten the day by imagining someone finding it decades later when the vehicle was repaired or restored.

It was a good ruse, but I would have preferred a time capsule or something more informative. Frowning, I set the paper aside, and because I couldn't let things lie, I went about dismantling the rest of the cupboard. I found nothing, and ended up making more work for myself, but it was easy enough to put everything back in place, my curiosity sated. Once done, and with the cupboard in fine repair, I sat for a moment as I couldn't help feeling that something wasn't quite right about this. Was it a joke, or was someone asking for help? If they were, why would they hide the message like this? Could it be that the person who did the work was in trouble way back when, and this was the only opportunity they had to send a message? If so, it was rather pointless, as who would see it?

Or was he expecting a colleague to see it because several people worked on the vehicle simultaneously? No, that was nonsense, right?

Tutting at my own gullible nature, I sniggered at my desperate need for intrigue. The investigating had turned me into a paranoid amateur sleuth finding mystery wherever I went, even if there was no mystery to be found.

"Hello?" called Erin from outside. She poked her head inside the camper and asked, "Are you decent?"

"It's too late if I'm not," I said with a smile and a wink.

"What you got there?" she asked with a raised eyebrow.

"Just a very old, and very lame joke," I said, tucking the paper into an open drawer then closing it.

"Um, okay. So, I hear you got bashed over the head? And Rhys told you about his trip to the station? You okay?"

"Fine, and I'm glad Rhys did the right thing."

"Me too. I appreciate this, Max. You've been a true friend to us both."

"It's no bother. Fancy a cuppa before we go? I'm parched this morning. Lack of sleep, I think."

"Sure, that sounds great. But first, how do I look? I nipped in to work for an hour, but now I have the whole day off. It's nice to wear my own clothes all day."

"You look great. Same as always. You like those striped tops, don't you? With the ripped jeans and the chains and things in your ears and around your neck, you're quite intimidating."

"Thanks!" she beamed, her warm smile and pretty face belying the scruffy, grunge style. But it somehow worked perfectly, and I was tempted to go get my ears pierced, but figured I'd most likely end up with my nose done, too, and before long it would be nipples, and then where would it end? I shuddered.

"What's up?"

"Nothing. Just thinking about nipples."

There was a very awkward, very prolonged silence as we both stared at each other.

"Anyone's in particular?" she asked with a wicked grin and a lick of the lips.

"I... It was the piercings. And I thought about getting my nipples pierced and..." I flung my hands into the air and laughed. "Sorry, I'm acting like a juvenile. I wasn't thinking about your nipples. Promise."

"Bet you are now though, right?" she teased.

"Absolutely not! I'm an ex-married man," I said in a fake huff. "Sorry if I caused offence."

"Max, chill out. I know you're a sound bloke. It's refreshing to meet a gentleman for a change. Even if he does keep banging on about nipples."

"I do not bang on about nipples!" I shouted.

"Did someone say nipples?" asked a passerby from the other side of the hedge.

"Marty Jones, you get on about your business or I'll tell your mum you nicked sweets from the shop."

"I never did," squealed the lad. Footsteps receded as the kid hurried away.

"I keep forgetting there's a path the other side of the garden. Silly, as I drive up here."

"So keep your voice down when you're talking dirty," Erin said playfully.

"I promise," I said with a wink.

After coffee, and once I'd recovered from embarrassment, we set off to see what the day would bring. The list of people to talk to was very short. Just Pip, the nurse from the clinic, and Patrick, the poached vet. We decided to visit Patrick first, hoping he'd be at home as the clinic was still closed down after Leo's murder.

He lived several miles out of town, so I drove us there with Anxious buckled up in the back. He lived in a modest, but very well-maintained cottage nestled into a beautiful hill painted in purple heather where sheep grazed and small ground birds launched into the air, chattering as we interrupted their peace as Vee chugged up the hill.

The whitewashed stone cottage was covered in clematis. Gaudy orange, red, and yellow specimens festooned the front wall, while the typical seaside hydrangeas were a riot of blue because of the acidic soil. Pots of shade-loving ferns and hostas flourished on the cooler north side of the house that we passed as Erin opened the gate and we approached the front door. The front garden was large, not a blade of grass to be seen. Instead, it was a wildlife haven with deep flowering borders, several ponds, and winding gravel paths where verbena cast a cheery hello, highlighted against grinning orange rudbeckia. Lamb's-ears were weighed down by fat bumblebees, the sound so loud it was like a chainsaw.

"He likes his gardening, I assume?" I asked.

"If he's not working with animals, he's working in his garden. He's been here for years. Bought it back when old cottages were cheap. Those days are long gone now, even around here."

"What's he like? We haven't spoken about him much."

"He's a nice guy. A bit abrupt, takes a while to warm to people, but nice. It's a shame he left, as he knows animals inside out, but I don't hold it against him. He has a house to run, and was just thinking of his future when he took Leo up on the offer."

"But Pip thinks differently?"

"Yeah. She's intense at times. She absolutely refuses to forgive him for leaving us, and you know about the fight they had?"

"It sounded rough. And I saw what happened yesterday. She's feisty, for sure."

"Feisty?" laughed Erin. "She's nuts at times. Come on, let's go around the back. He's hardly ever inside."

Erin led the way around the cottage and down another shady path brimming with more ferns and shade-loving plants like Japanese anemone and a huge clump of Calla lilies, the white trumpet-like blooms easily six feet tall. I felt transported into another world, and when we turned the corner into the back garden I thought for a moment I truly had been beamed to another part of the planet.

The garden wasn't large, maybe fifty feet long by forty wide—although it was hard to tell because of how densely it was planted—but the ancient stone walls gave me a rough idea.

Where the front was all flowers and cheer, the rear was a tropical paradise with only a hint of colour. Limited to red and orange flowers, the incredible garden relied on every shade of green imaginable and an endless variety of leaf shapes and sizes to spark jaw-dropping interest.

"Hello," said the man I assumed was Patrick, although I was more concerned about the massive machete he was gripping tightly as he scowled at us.

Chapter 16

"How you doing, Patrick?" said Erin brightly. "Um, that looks kinda dangerous. You got a licence for that?"

Patrick locked his smouldering brown eyes on me for a moment—and yes, they were smouldering, even I could see that—then glanced down to the machete. "Oh, sorry, I was hacking back the gunnera. It's gone rogue and is taking over the entire garden. Only thing that works is this old thing. Let me put it down." Patrick placed the gardening tool on a compact cast-iron table then turned back to us and asked, "Max, I presume?" with a raised eyebrow that I could tell made women gasp because that's exactly what Erin did.

Patrick was lean, as tall as me at six one, tanned, with a jaw so square it was bordering on ridiculous. His manicured stubble would have made George Michael run screaming for the hills in frustration. But it didn't end there. He was wide-shouldered like a swimmer, had full lips that were almost as red as Erin's, long eyelashes that somehow made me think of a camel, but a damn handsome one. His cut-offs were frayed just so, and the red and white check shirt was unbuttoned enough to reveal dense chest muscles.

"You're the vet?" I asked. "Not a male model?"

"I wish!" beamed Patrick, brushing a curly lock from his eyes.

"Max!" warned Erin. "Are you gushing over Patrick?"

"I'm simply saying he's a very handsome guy. That's alright, isn't it? Is it weird? Am I being weird?"

"You are now," said Erin with a frown.

"Yes, mate, a bit weird," chuckled Patrick as he stepped forward and we shook hands. He hugged Erin and she reciprocated, and it seemed she'd been honest about her feelings—she didn't hold a grudge and he was a genuinely nice bloke.

"Sorry about that. I guess I was expecting..."

"An Ollie!" they both interrupted, laughing.

"Yes, someone who looks more like Ollie. I mean, he looks like a vet. You look like, er, something different."

"I get it all the time," said Patrick. "I'm different when I'm in my white overcoat and sticking my finger up a dog's bum."

Anxious whined and took a step away from Patrick. He'd already been acting cautious as he could probably smell the vet-vibe on him, but now he was certain this was not a man to get too close too.

"Don't be so coy," said Erin. "We all know you're ridiculously hot." She turned to me and said, "He's like you. He doesn't see it in himself."

"Me?" I asked. "I know Min says I'm fanciable, and that you said I was nice-looking, but there's no comparison."

"Mate, you're a hunk," agreed Patrick. "Wow, what is wrong with us? We know the best-looking out of everyone is Erin."

"True," I said.

Erin blushed cutely and bowed, then said, "Thanks, guys. Now, do we get a cuppa, or do we have to help with the gardening first?"

"Sure, of course. Sorry, that was rude of me. What'll it be?"

We both wanted tea, so Patrick disappeared through a tiny back door and left us in the garden.

I told Erin I needed to make a call, so excused myself, had a quick chat and managed to clear up a question that had been bothering me, then returned a moment later.

"What are you looking so smug about?"

"Nothing," I said, unable to stop smiling.

"Ah, I get it. This is about last night and you trying to set Rhys up with someone, isn't it? Be warned, he's quite shy without the beer, and I'm not sure it's a great idea. He's been on a few blind dates with women I know and it never worked out. He's quite fussy. Who is it?"

"All shall be revealed. Oh, and I almost forgot. Happy birthday." I handed Erin the card signed by me and Anxious.

"How did you know? Ah, Rhys told you. Thank you, Max, but you didn't have to go to any trouble. Especially after what happened to you."

"It was no trouble."

Erin read the card, then looked up with a grin and said, "I'm not sure who has the worst handwriting. You, or Anxious."

"That's not a fair comparison! I have to write more words. He only ever learned one."

Erin kissed me on the cheek and bent to stroke Anxious' head as he sat waiting patiently for his thanks.

Patrick arrived just then, with a tray of mugs of tea, a plate of chocolate biscuits, and a card for Erin.

"Happy birthday."

"Patrick, thank you. You remembered?"

"Of course I did. I was going to post it, as I wasn't sure if I should come around, but then I figured I hadn't seen you for a while so would deliver it later."

"You're welcome any time, you know that. I'm sorry we haven't seen much of each other, but it's been busy lately, not that it's your fault," she added hurriedly, "and now all this carnage."

"I understand. I'm an outcast and now you both suspect me of murder. That's why you're here, isn't it? To sound me out, see if I had anything to do with it?"

"No. Absolutely not!" blurted Erin.

"Yes, that's it exactly," I said honestly. Erin gave me the evil eye, but I shrugged. "Patrick isn't daft. It's obvious why we're here. Patrick, do you mind if we ask you some questions? I'm guessing you know I'm looking into this?"

"Word gets around. I'm not quite sure why some ex-chef living in a van is involved in a murder enquiry, but shoot. Ask away. I have nothing to hide."

"Thanks. And as to why, it's just become obvious to me that this is my calling. Things keep happening as I travel around, and I can't ignore it, so I try to help. You okay with that?"

"Sure, it's very honourable. But I've already spoken to the police on multiple occasions, so I don't know what else I can add."

"Why did you go and work for Leo rather than stay with Ollie?"

"That's an easy question to answer and a very difficult one," he said quietly.

"Why?" asked Erin. "It's because Leo and the people behind him offered more money and the chance to be a partner one day, isn't it?"

"That was part of it, yes. But it was more than that."

"Was it because of Pip?" I asked.

"No. We were doing fine until I got the offer from Leo, and then we were arguing constantly. She refused to see my side of things and it got out of control. I never realised she had such a temper until I refused to do as she said. She'd lost control once before, but that time at the clinic when she broke my nose was the final straw. There was no coming back from that. Domestic violence is a serious matter and I would never, ever dream of hitting a woman. It goes both ways, and what she did was inexcusable."

"So that was the end of the relationship? Once you told her you were leaving to work for Leo?" I asked.

"Yes, and we haven't spoken since. I was willing to be civil to her once things cooled down, but she point-blank refused. Pip's as stubborn as they come in some regards, and very loyal to her friends. Shame she didn't show me the same loyalty or understanding."

"What was the other reason?" I asked. "You said it was complicated? What else made you decide to leave?"

Patrick sipped his tea, eyes downcast, then he met both our eyes and said, "Ollie."

"Ollie?" asked Erin, spitting tea.

"Yes. Look, Erin, I don't want to badmouth anyone, and you know I'm not that kind of guy, but Ollie isn't what he seems."

"He's a sweetheart. He's looked after us all these years, done whatever he can for us, and runs the practice like a pro. What was your beef with him?"

"No beef as such, just sometimes he was off. It's hard to describe, but sometimes I got a feeling about him. Like something wasn't quite right. Sure, he's amicable and friendly, sometimes too friendly, so I could never figure out what was wrong about our relationship. We didn't argue as such, but he made it clear who was in charge."

"He is in charge! It's his practice."

"Yes, I know, which is why this is so awkward to explain. I kept getting this feeling about him. Like something wasn't quite right and the pressure was building for him. It was the oddest thing. With both of us seeing to the animals, things were running smoothly, but there was this intensity with him sometimes when we were alone, as though he was about to blow his top."

"He's just highly strung," said Erin. "He feels the stress of looking after the animals as well as the staff. It's a lot of responsibility."

"Like I said, it's difficult to explain. Max, you understand, don't you?"

"I do," I said, sipping my tea while I thought this over properly. "Sometimes you get a vibe about someone and you know to be on your guard. That something isn't right and there's more to the person than they show others. You become unsettled and can't wait to get out of their company. You don't know why, just that it won't end well."

"Max, how do you know all that?" asked Erin.

"Because I was in charge of numerous kitchens over the years, or worked under others, and now and then you come across someone who, to put it bluntly, creeps you out. You don't know why, but if you let your intuition guide you, you make sure to steer well clear. I've had several people like that, and it never ended well."

"What did you do?" asked Patrick, leaning forward.

"I fired them."

"Max! That's awful."

"No, it isn't. Kitchens, like veterinary practices, are high stress environments, and people need to keep a level head and control themselves. The first few times I didn't follow my gut and it ended up with the person going off the rails and almost killing someone when they threw a pan of hot oil at a colleague who'd annoyed them. The other time it was a knife. I vowed there and then to always follow my instincts, and if I got a bad feeling about someone, and I don't mean I didn't like them, I mean if I thought they were going to blow, then I fired them. They always deserved it, as when I let them go they showed their true selves."

"That's the right call," said Patrick. "And that's how I felt. How I still feel about Ollie. Something wasn't right, so when I got the offer I had to take it. Erin, I'm sorry I left you all behind, but I didn't know what to do. And now look what's happened. I told the police all this, but they dismissed it like I was a fool. It was awful."

"You can't possibly think Ollie was involved in this?" said Erin, aghast. "He would never do such a thing. And besides, he was with Max in the consulting room. He couldn't have done it."

"He could," I admitted.

"But you were with him."

"I was with him when the gas went off and certainly when everyone was hit over the head. We were in the room together with Anxious when that happened, and when the animals were taken. But Ollie was in the waiting room when Riley was stabbed. It was full of smoke and impossible to see, so, in theory anyone could have actually committed the murder. And as for Leo, he was murdered the next day late at night behind his car, so that could have been absolutely anyone too."

"Max, you can't be serious?" Erin shook her head, unwilling to even consider it.

"I'm not saying I suspect him. In fact, I don't. But it's possible. There's some other person involved in this, that's obvious, so maybe Ollie played a part to kill Riley, or used his death as an excuse to get Leo out of the way."

"He wouldn't kill a member of staff so he could go on to eliminate Leo. That's nuts."

"I know it's far-fetched. I'm just talking about the possibility of it."

"No, I refuse to believe it. Patrick, tell him that Ollie would never do that."

"I'm sorry, but I can't. As I said, I left because something didn't feel right between me and Ollie. What that was I don't know, but it was definitely there."

"And now I want to ask about Pip. I'm sorry about all this, but I've got the feeling things are coming to a head. Patrick, someone attacked me late last night, and I'm sure this will be over soon one way or another."

"Are you okay?"

"Fine, but it was scary. Could Pip have done this? Is there any reason why she would?"

"She's wild, and has a temper, but like I said, she's loyal to Ollie and would never harm his business."

"Even if she knew he'd recover once she eliminated Leo. Ollie's place was rammed with people yesterday, so he's come out on top now your place is closed for a while. Maybe that's the motive?"

"We'll bounce back. The owners of the company just wanted to close for a few days out of a sign of respect, but we're opening again tomorrow. I'll be in charge, and we'll find another to take my place, but I'll be the manager now. And yes, I know that looks bad for me, but I swear I had nothing to do with any of this."

"I appreciate the honesty," I said, finishing my tea. "Now, are you going to show me around this incredible garden of yours?"

Patrick brightened as he jumped to his feet and said, "Absolutely. There's nothing I enjoy more than showing off my hard work."

It was over an hour later when we emerged from Patrick's tropical garden, the shade of the unusual, fast-growing specimens welcome, the moss and running water a delight, the fact he'd managed to cram so much in and yet make it feel so much larger than it was truly astounding.

We said our goodbyes and Erin promised to stay in touch, then retreated to the campervan where we sat for a moment to gather our thoughts.

"Do you really think Ollie might have done this?" she asked sadly. "I can't bear to think he was involved."

"He seems like a nice guy to me, and has been very helpful, so I don't think so, no. But we can't dismiss what Patrick said either. He was clearly reluctant to leave you all, but things between him and Ollie were reaching breaking point as far as he was concerned. He risked his relationship and friendships for what he thought was right, so what do you make of that?"

"I have no clue!" declared Erin, laughing nervously as she shook her head. "Max, how do you figure these things out? It's impossible."

"We'll get there. You asked a lot of good questions, and we're getting closer. We need to visit Pip next, but before we do, what can you tell me about Riley? Either he was killed by accident, or just to cause a distraction, or he was killed on purpose and that means a motive. What was he like?"

"Just a regular fella," shrugged Erin. "Kinda quiet, didn't mix too much with everyone as he had his own thing going on, but very good at his job and he was always working. He put in a lot of hours, really stepped up when Patrick left, but he was a nurse, not a vet, so there was only so much he could do to help Ollie out."

"No enemies? No arguments you can recall? Anything that he might have said that might make him a target?"

"Nothing. He just did his job and kept his head down. A quiet guy with no enemies, as most of us don't, do we?"

"No, we don't."

"Max, he was just a regular guy. There's no reason why he would be killed. It makes no sense at all."

"Was he married? A girlfriend? Boyfriend? Are his parents local?"

"He was single. He lived alone. He's not from the area, so we can't visit his parents, and I don't think that would be right anyway. I guess if we really wanted to we could make the drive, but what could they say?"

"You're right. It would be an intrusion. I'm sure the police have spoken to them anyway. Now, what about Pip?"

"What about her?"

"Do you trust her?"

"Absolutely. She's lovely, despite what Patrick said. I've only ever seen her lose her tempter twice. Once with him, and then with Leo. Apart from that, she's like a pussycat. Softly spoken, although she takes no nonsense, just like me, and an excellent nurse. She's amazing with the animals, and works harder than any of us as she runs the kennels as well as doing everything else. She's just lovely. I can't reconcile how she was with Patrick with the woman I know."

"Then that right there is an issue, isn't it? I can tell you're concerned about this. If she's so nice, she shouldn't blow her top like that."

"No, she shouldn't. It's like she's two entirely different people."

"And one of them had a real grudge against both Patrick and Leo."

"You think she organised all this to get back at them? Well, it hasn't worked very well as now Patrick's going to get a promotion."

"So maybe we need to keep an eye on him. Look out for him. Or maybe we need to see what Pip is really made of, and watch how she reacts when he's around."

"What are you thinking?" she asked with a curious smile.

"Let's just say I have an idea for later, but for now let's just go and pay her a visit. Will she mind?"

"I asked her this morning and she said it was fine. She wants this solved just like we all do."

"Then let's go have a chat."

Chapter 17

Pip's place was not what I expected. For some reason, I'd imagined a meticulously neat, compact property, possibly even an apartment on one of the new developments a few miles from town; it was the complete opposite. After climbing up into the hills, the grass making way for tough scrub and spiky reeds in the boggy ground, we hit a narrow dirt track. Ruined old farmhouses looked romantic on such a lovely day, but belied the harshness of the climate during the winter and the fact that many had abandoned such a remote existence in favour of an easier life.

"She lives out here?" I asked.

"Just up ahead. Think we'll make it?"

"Barely. But the old girl's coping so far."

We hit a deep pothole and bounced about in our seats. Something crunched underneath, making me wince.

Around the bend, we turned off onto an even worse track, then I parked the other side of the farm gate, not wanting to risk turning in the cramped yard full of tractors and vehicles any scrapyard would think twice about taking.

The moment I let Anxious out he darted off, barking, so we hurried after him then waved as Pip emerged from an outbuilding, cradling a stack of split wood.

"Hey," she beamed.

We said our hellos, Anxious getting antsy because he couldn't have a fuss from his new favourite nurse, actually, the only one he had ever taken a shine to, so Pip said, "Let me dump this lot, then we can have a chat. And sorry, Anxious, I'll be with you in a moment." Pip vanished inside the squat stone cottage, then emerged a moment later, slapping her hands on her grubby jeans to clean them up a little.

"Firewood?" I asked. "Bit warm for that, isn't it?"

"Some of these old cottages just never dry out. We need to make repairs to the roof and gutters, but who has the time? The damp gets into the walls and is a bugger to dry out. We run fires almost every day of the year." Pip shrugged; it was what it was.

"Makes sense. Um, I think someone needs a fuss," I hinted.

"Oh, Anxious, I'm sorry. Gosh, is your paw still hurting?" Pip bent to give the desperate-looking trickster a big cuddle because he was currently holding his leg high and looking about as mournful as if I'd forgotten both breakfast and dinner.

"He's such a sneak," I sighed. "He's been racing all over the place and is absolutely fine. You shouldn't cry wolf, Anxious, or nobody will believe you when you're really poorly."

Completely unheeding my words, Anxious was agog with excitement for some reason, tail wagging manically and utterly crazed. He began to lick Pip's chin and get rather wild, but she knew how to handle dogs and laughed it off then stood and ignored him until he wandered off to sniff around.

"We won't take up much of your time, as it looks like you're busy, but I wanted to clear a few things up. Is that okay?"

"Sure, no problem," she said breezily, smiling.

"And so you know honesty goes both ways, we've just come from Patrick's."

Pip's demeanour changed instantly. Her fine pale features, cupped by a short, dark, very straight bob haircut, turned ugly as she frowned and her fists bunched. "That snake. What'd he have to say for himself?"

"Not much, actually. Just that he wished things had turned out differently."

"Me too. I'm sorry I hit him. I truly am. I'm getting help for my temper. I wish I'd never done it, but I'm hot-headed and protective."

"We know that," soothed Erin. "Pip, is there anything you can tell us that you haven't already said? Anything at all?"

Pip rubbed at her cheek and thought before saying, "No, nothing. It happened just as I already said. Nobody could see, and I was the last out into the waiting room. Riley was already dead, you and Aggie were behind the counter, and she had that red rubber toy in her mouth. That was weird, wasn't it? Who would do that? Although, it did mean Aggie was quiet for a while, right? Sorry, that was in bad taste, but you know what she's like. She can't keep quiet for two seconds, and she's just so loud."

"She sure is," I chuckled. "But was there anything else you saw? You were coming from the back where there was less smoke, so maybe you noticed something that doesn't fit?"

"Like what?"

"I have no idea," I conceded.

"There really was nothing. I was focused on the shouts of everyone, then on poor Riley. I didn't see anything."

"Okay, then let me ask you this? Who do you think it was? Be honest. It's not like we're going to arrest you for having an opinion."

"I figured it was Leo until he was killed. And yes, I regret attacking him, too, but not that much." Pip smiled, clearly not at all sorry for sending him on his way after gloating over Ollie's troubles.

"Who else? What about Ollie?"

"Max! You can't say that," warned Erin. "It absolutely wasn't Ollie."

"Why would you think that for a moment?" asked Pip.

"It's just that we heard he might have been acting strangely lately. Out of sorts. Maybe there was more going on than we thought?"

"He's stressed about the future. With Patrick leaving, it put him in a dodgy situation. And the new clinic took a lot of our customers. It's not a good time. Although, now things are looking up again. I think they would have come back anyway. They just took advantage of the special introductory offer for cheap consultations, but from what people were saying yesterday, they regretted it. No, we'll be fine. Everything is great again now."

"Because two men are dead," I reminded her.

"Yes, I know, but one of them was a truly horrible man. I tell it like it is, Max, that's my style, and I know it rubs some people up the wrong way, but they'll just have to deal with it. I'm not sorry Leo's dead, but I am sorry he was murdered. Do you suspect me?"

"A little," I admitted.

"Fair enough. Now, I think we're done here, don't you? Max, I get where you're coming from, but trust me, you're barking up the wrong tree. I would do anything to protect those I care about, and that includes you, Erin, but murder? Come on!"

"We're sorry to be so blunt, aren't we, Max?" said Erin as she nudged me in the ribs and raised an eyebrow. "We don't really think it was you. At least, I don't."

"No, neither do I."

"Why so sure?" asked Pip.

"Because there is no way Anxious would like you as much if you were the killer. I trust him more than I trust myself."

Pip grinned, then hugged Erin, and then, much to my surprise, she hugged me too. When she released me, she stepped back and asked, "Friends?"

"Yes, friends. And sorry for putting you on the spot like this. I really am just trying to help."

"I get it, and thank you. I'll see you soon?" she asked with a wink.

Remembering the paintball this evening, I said, "Yes, very soon," and winked back.

We both laughed, leaving Erin looking puzzled as I called for Anxious. He had another fuss, then we left Pip to her chores.

As we drove off, Erin asked, "What was that about at the end? You two were all smiles and winks."

"Nothing," I said, stony-faced.

"Hmm."

"She's genuine, isn't she? No-nonsense, but genuine?"

"Absolutely. I like Pip a lot. You just have to know how to deal with her. One thing's for certain, she had nothing to do with any of this."

"Nothing's certain. Of that I'm sure," I teased.

Erin giggled, then turned serious. "So, who could it be? Who would commit such a horrid crime?"

"We have a rather long list, but I'm pretty sure I know who it was now."

"Who? Come on, tell me?"

"I don't want to jump the gun on this, Erin, and to be honest it's little more than a hunch. I have more snooping around to do later, but you'll find out soon enough."

"Spoilsport," she sulked.

"It's best I don't say anything more, because if I do you'll act differently, and that might mean we'll never get to the truth. Understand?"

Erin shrugged. "I'm not bothered anyway."

"Liar!" I said, shaking my head and smiling.

"Okay, maybe I am a teensy bit bothered. You really can't tell me?"

"Not yet. Let me think it over and ask around some more, but I'm certain everything's coming together. It's a shock. I can tell you that much."

"Max, are you doing this on purpose to wind me up? You can't leave me hanging like this."

"I'm sorry, but it's for the best. I promise that by tonight all will be revealed."

"Oh, you mean after my 'surprise' at Paintball in the Hills?" she asked with a wicked grin.

"You know about that?"

"My brother is about as good at keeping secrets as you are at cutting your hair," she giggled. "I probably knew before he did. I left him enough hints. And I don't mean subtle ones. He thinks he's planned a big surprise, but I've been planting the idea in his head for days. It's a good way to blow off steam, and boy do we all need that. But there's more," she said, suddenly fidgeting with a rip in her jeans.

"Do tell," I said, already suspecting she had the exact same idea as me.

"I figured if we can get everyone together, and put them in a stressful situation, even though it is just paintball, something might happen. We might get some insight."

"That's exactly what I thought once Rhys told me about it. So, you don't mind if we invite Patrick as well? I know he and Pip aren't getting on, but we need all the players together. Or, as many as we can get."

"I was going to call him later. He'll come, don't worry. So, now we'll have me, you, Rhys, Pip, Patrick, Ollie, Aggie, her gross husband Kent, and I know you called Cindy as you think she's a great match for Rhys."

"How could you possibly know that?" I asked, impressed.

"Because I was going to do it. I've been thinking about him a lot lately, and she's perfect for him."

"I called her," I admitted. "You aren't worried about the fact she knocked Riley out?"

"Whatever that was about, I'm sure she had her reasons. People fight, but it doesn't mean they turn an argument into murder. Cindy's cool."

"Anyone else?"

"I think that's it."

"Me too. We can rule out the other pet owners, I think. Cindy is really nice, but there's something different about her. I'm not saying it was her. In fact, I don't think it was. But she might help to liven things up."

"But you aren't saying it was one of us, are you? What about the other people you've spoken to?"

"I can't very well invite them all. And besides, someone in this group knows something. Maybe they don't know they know, but they do. If nothing else, this will help us figure out who the true killer is. Plus, we have the guys at Paintball in the Hills. This is the perfect way to get closer to them. The fact the smoke grenades came from there means it's all linked, right?"

"You think it could be one of them?"

"Like I said, it's best I don't give too much away. And I still haven't talked to your ex-boyfriend."

"I told you, it wasn't him. He isn't like that."

"Then let's just wait and see what happens."

"Man, this is going to be gnarly!" beamed Erin.

"Gnarly? I hope not."

Erin shook her head and leaned back, oozing a knowing, smug satisfaction. "Trust me, it will be."

I dropped Erin at home. She was going to pamper herself by relaxing for the afternoon on the beach before taking a nice bath, then would meet everyone at Paintball in the Hills at six. I offered to make an early dinner, but she said she wanted to just see how the day went and not have to race around. I understood, and got the impression she needed some quiet time after all the stress.

I parked in town and wandered down the alley to the scene of Leo's murder, not surprised to find there was no sign of the grisly death. Kent's van was parked by the wall, with several other vehicles taking up the other spots, and I wondered whether I should pay him and Aggie another visit but thought better of it.

Anxious sniffed around the vehicles, but soon got bored, so I made a mental image of which back gardens led to which houses, then traced the route out onto the roads and began knocking on doors. Surprisingly, most people were at home, the population rather elderly and enjoying their retirement in such a picturesque town. I drank more tea and ate more custard creams than was sensible, and Anxious practically waddled from door to door, smug as only a dog who knows he's cute and has a poorly paw ace up his bandaged sleeve to play to ensure he got even more treats than me.

Everyone was very helpful, if rather keen to gossip, but several hours later, and after hearing about all manner of medical conditions, problems with the neighbours, rants about the council, complaints regards bin collections, and arguments over parking, I finally had all I needed to be sure my hunch was correct and I knew who the despicable culprit was.

Now all that was left to do was wait.

And eat.

Chapter 18

After a very early and light dinner, Anxious and I dressed appropriately for paintball. Meaning, he went as he was born, and I wore sturdy boots, black combat trousers, and a black shirt with the sleeves rolled up.

The short drive there took no time at all, even with the usual roadworks signs, the temporary traffic lights, and not a single workman or hole dug.

After parking, we made our way to the orientation area to find everyone already there and waiting.

"Sorry, are we late?" I asked.

"Nope, but everyone else is early," said Dai, eyes never still as he studied each of us in turn. He brushed his wild tangle of hair from his tanned face, smiled, then added, "Right, let's get you kitted out, then we'll go over the guns and how to maximise the fun you're about to have. Help yourselves to the gear. We have all sizes." He pointed to several crates of combat vests, goggles, helmets, and pads for knees and elbows, saying the pads were optional.

As everyone sorted through the sizes, I asked if Anxious was allowed to join in.

Dai beamed and said, "Of course. My dogs love chasing around, but it can be dangerous, so let me see what I can find." He disappeared into the wooden hut, then emerged a moment later and bent beside Anxious.

"Now, if you want to play paintball, you have to wear this gear. That okay?"

Anxious looked to me, I nodded, so he stood still while Dai fixed a tiny combat vest with straps under his belly, adjusted it so his torso was protected, then snapped on a small pair of goggles.

Dai stood back and grunted in satisfaction. "Looks good. Like a right little trooper."

"Very smart," I told Anxious, stifling a giggle.

"No gun?" I asked Dai.

"No gun," he grinned.

Anxious paraded around in front of us as we got ready, and once our helmets were on and goggles in place, Dai demonstrated the various weapons and how to load them, showed us the paintballs and how much mess they made by shooting at a tree, then explained the rules of the game.

It was very simple. There would be two teams, each with a flag at home base. The idea was to capture the opposing team's flag. If you got shot, you were out for the round, of which there would be five, so you had to make use of the tree cover, hide behind the various forts, use the tree houses for ambushes, and generally run around like nutters shouting and screaming while your heart hammered in your chest even though you knew it was just make-believe war.

Dai left us to split into teams, which consisted of me, Erin, Rhys, Patrick, and Cindy, with our opponents being Ollie, Aggie, Kent, and Pip. Anxious was team three, which made him feel special, and his job was to run around like a lunatic, barking at everyone and giving away their positions, which he did a fine job of accomplishing, much to everyone's dismay.

The first game was absolute carnage. Erin, Rhys, and Ollie knew what they were doing, but they weren't exactly team players and kept running off and using all the hides they knew about from past experience, leaving the rest of us to take up the rear. Aggie and Kent weren't exactly fast on their feet, but Kent was an ace shot and took out Patrick in just a few minutes, much to his dismay, but then Cindy got a shot at him and he was out too.

Pip made up for her lack of skill with pure anger, and whizzed from tree to tree, firing randomly as she went, until she got taken out by me of all people with a lucky shot.

The game ended ten minutes later with Ollie's team the victors. Everyone was already covered in red and blue paint spatters, but we were laughing and having a great time. Pip cast a few stern scowls at Patrick, but even she was caught up in the fun and hadn't tried to single him out, which was good.

Kent kept rubbing at his knee, complaining about it being an old war wound and laughing, but nobody asked for more details and I felt that was probably for the best. Aggie was holding her own, no more winded than the rest of us. Cindy hadn't even broken a sweat, clearly still very fit, and was by far the most experienced in combat because of her army days. She and Rhys talked a lot, so at least one plan had worked flawlessly, and Erin and I exchanged a few knowing looks as they huddled close and laughed.

The next few rounds were pretty even, one win each, but round four was considerably slower. With Cindy coming into her own because of her superior fitness, we easily won with the others getting a thorough thrashing.

Now it was two flag captures each, with everything to play for. After a drink and a quick snack of a banana and biscuits for the energy, we were raring to go, only if it meant it would soon be over and we could rest up.

With the flags planted, we took our positions. Cindy was the most accurate, so she raced ahead and up into a tree house while the rest of us lay down suppressing fire. Once she was safe, we advanced cautiously, Anxious leading the way as he couldn't be eliminated. He was covered in paint blobs, wearing them like a badge of honour, in no way hindered by the snug combat vest.

We fanned out, confident, only to receive a warning from Cindy that the enemy were advancing. We scattered, heading for the trees, and I narrowly missed getting caught in a crossfire that focused on Patrick, who was pinned down then eliminated after a particularly savage attack from the right. Pip emerged from behind a makeshift wooden barrier, grinning as she lifted her goggles and glared at him.

"Serves you right. Traitor," she hissed, her face a mask of hatred.

She turned at a sound and realised I'd seen her, so raced away, pulling her goggles down.

"Still not besties then?" I asked.

"Not quite. But at least she didn't throttle me," Patrick sighed. "I'll wait back at our flag."

Erin cheered as a very blue Kent left the cover of the trees, hands up. Laughing his defeat off, he limped over to our flag to join Patrick. Aggie darted past, firing at me, but missed, so I let off a few shots but they went wide too.

Cindy continued to hold down the enemy from her vantage point, and soon enough Pip was taken out. She took it surprisingly well, and congratulated Cindy on her excellent marksmanship. Numbers were dwindling fast, but there was still all to play for, and much pride at stake, so we forged ahead, Erin and Rhys keeping low and firing at Ollie and Aggie as they tried to reach the enemy stronghold.

I saw my chance and rushed forward, narrowly missing a skilled shot by Ollie, then slid to the dirt and hid behind a fort, nursing my scraped knees as Anxious bounded onto my lap, agog with pleasure at finally finding a game everyone enjoyed as much as him. I'd have to bring him once a year as a treat for his birthday.

Incensed by missing what should have been a straightforward shot, Ollie charged after me, face grim, then ducked behind a rusty car and fired through the missing windows. Anxious took a hit to the side, but just ran over and barked happily at Ollie, who tried to shoo him away, believing I hadn't seen him.

With Anxious distracting him, I surged ahead, the flag in my sights, but I was so intent on capturing their flag that I'd forgotten about our own, and who was guarding it, if anyone?

Turning, I sighed as I spied Aggie loping along with her gun over her shoulder. She dashed ahead as her teammates encouraged her. I turned and sprinted back, shouting to Erin and Rhys to hurry up and get the other flag, then fired at Aggie just as she reached the platform. I got a lucky shot and hit her square in the back, and she turned, scowling, just as Cindy shot her again in the chest for good measure.

With a whoop from the far end of the compound, Erin emerged from the platform, red-faced and beaming, with Rhys by her side, the flag in her hands.

"We did it!" she shouted, waving the flag high for all to see. "We won!"

"Yes!" I cheered, fist pumping the air with excitement.

Anxious yipped wildly, then raced over to Erin. She removed the flag from the pole, stuck it into his combat vest, and together they sauntered over, joined by Cindy as she jumped from the tree house like a panther.

Together, we climbed up onto the platform to join the others, beaming at our teammates who slapped us heartily on the back and congratulated everyone for a job well done.

"Let's get some space," said Ollie sourly. "There isn't enough room for us on this wonky platform."

Erin and I exchanged a look as everyone followed Ollie to the designated finish point, where we each stood with our team like we were sworn enemies.

"That was fun," I said to break the stony silence. "Did everyone have a good time?"

"It was awesome!" beamed Ollie. "Sorry for being grumpy when we played, but I take it quite seriously. I love paintball!"

"Me too," agreed Erin. "Everyone was amazing. Thank you all for coming. It's been a great birthday treat, and I owe it all to my brilliant brother." She kissed Rhys on the cheek, who beamed happily, maybe because of that, or maybe because Cindy was still right by his side and smiling at him adoringly.

"You cheated," accused Aggie, pointing at me.

"Me? I did no such thing. I got you in the back when you were running for the flag. That's fair. It's how you play." There were murmurs of agreement from my team, and a few words from Aggie's comrades explaining that I played the game right, but she wasn't happy.

"You shot me in the back like a coward."

"This is just a game, Aggie," soothed Ollie. "Everyone got shot in the back. It's what you do. Max just played along like everyone else."

"Well, I don't like it. It's cowardly." She glared at me, and it was then that I knew my hunch had been right. More than a hunch. I was certain.

"At least nobody killed anyone," joked Patrick, but nobody else laughed.

"Sorry, that was in bad taste. Perhaps this wasn't such a good idea? Maybe a bit too close to home?"

"No, it's fine," said Ollie. "We needed to unwind, and this did the job. But it is a shame we still haven't uncovered the murderer. The police have nothing, and the trail is going cold."

"They'll figure it out," said Aggie in her usual roar.

"It was so terrible," said Cindy. "If there's anything I can do to help, please just ask. Thank you for letting me play. It's been incredible to meet you all properly and feel included in something. But it would be nice if the killer was found."

"Maybe it was you," accused Pip. "You knocked Riley out, and now he's dead. It's a bit suspicious that you won't tell anyone what it was about, isn't it?" she sneered.

"Leave her alone," growled Rhys.

"Cindy's not the killer," insisted Erin.

"How do you know?" snapped Pip.

"It wasn't what you think," said Cindy softly.

"Then explain yourself!" demanded Pip.

"Riley asked me out. He wasn't my type, so I politely turned him down. He seemed fine about it, if a little embarrassed, and I thought that was that. But then he said something disparaging, probably because he felt awkward, and I saw red and floored him. But I didn't kill him."

"What did he say that was so bad?" asked Pip.

"He said I looked too much like a man anyway. Because of my muscles. I punched him and stormed off. That was it. Not a nice thing to do, I know, but I was so angry."

"I think you're beautiful," said Rhys, blushing.

"That's so sweet," said Cindy, smiling.

"So that means we really still haven't found the killer?" asked Pip, nodding at Cindy as she mouthed a silent apology.

"They have been found," I said, suddenly feeling nervous now it was crunch time. I took a deep breath as everyone gasped, then went for it. "I'm sorry about this, but it has to be done now. I know who did it, and have done since this morning."

"You can't possibly know," snapped Ollie, frowning, with his arms crossed.

"Why not?"

"Because... because how could you? It's certainly not any of us. So why are we listening to you?"

"Ollie, that's not very nice," warned Erin.

"I'm sorry, but this has gone on long enough. Max, I know we asked you to help, that I asked you after learning about the other crimes you'd solved, but what could you possibly know that the detectives don't?"

"Like I said, I know who the killer is."

"Who? Go on then, tell us. Who's the hateful murderer?" he huffed.

I pointed at the two people next to Ollie and said, "It was them. Aggie and Kent."

Chapter 19

"Don't be ridiculous!" roared Aggie, her face so contorted in livid rage she appeared reptilian.

"That's my wife you're talking about," hissed Kent, stepping forward, fists bunched, his filthy jeans sagging dangerously low until he hitched them up.

"Max, you've got this all wrong," said Erin softly, placing a hand on my shoulder to stop me from continuing.

I shook my head. "I'm sorry, but I don't. I'm right, I know I am. Aggie and Kent are responsible. They did it all."

"This is beyond insulting," bellowed Aggie. "I'm leaving. Come on, Kent, we don't have to listen to this a moment longer."

"You're lucky these aren't real guns, or you'd be dead by now," warned Kent as he raised the paintball gun to my head and clicked the trigger. The chamber was empty, but the warning was clear enough.

"Nobody's going anywhere until they explain what on earth is going on," insisted Ollie as he stepped forward and stood between us. "Max, surely you don't believe it was Aggie? Kent, maybe, no offence," Kent grumbled but remained quiet, "but Aggie's in her sixties and a bird of a woman. Look at her. She's not frail, but she's not exactly burly either. She couldn't have done this. It's not possible."

"She could. And she did. Don't you all see? It's obvious now I think about it. Aggie had the perfect alibi and provided an airtight alibi for Kent. I thought it was him for a while after seeing him talking to Leo and then Leo being murdered, but Aggie vouched for him. It worked out perfectly for both of them."

"That's because we're innocent," said Kent.

"Yes, of course," said Ollie, placating Kent with a wave of his hand. "Nobody's accusing you of murder."

"He is," snarled Aggie. "He said me and my Kent did it. I've worked for you for years, and been at the practice for decades. I love the animals. I love all of you. And now you let this stranger talk to me like this? It's downright criminal, not to mention idiotic."

Everyone turned to me, a mixture of surprise, regret, or almost shame that they'd put their trust in me. It was clear they were concerned I'd done something awful and accused two innocent people.

"I'm sorry that you don't believe me, and I regret having to break the news like this, but it was the only way for me to be sure. When Rhys said about the paintball, I figured it was the perfect opportunity to get everyone together and finally let everything fall into place."

"Max, what are you talking about?" asked Rhys as he pulled off his goggles and wiped his sweaty brow.

"There's a lot of tension amongst you all. Pip hates Patrick, Patrick doesn't trust Ollie, Ollie's suspicious of Pip, Erin thinks everyone is great, which is nice, Cindy and Riley had a fight, and Rhys had the means to pull this off because of his dodgy mates. But then there's Aggie, who nobody suspects, who hasn't had a cross word with anyone, but her husband has a dark past."

"That was years ago and I'm totally reformed," insisted Kent.

"And I don't have a problem with Pip. She's a great worker," said Ollie.

"That's not true, and you know it," said Erin, her eyes widening in shock for speaking up. "You have had a few fallings out, and I've seen how you look at her sometimes. Afraid she'll blow, so you watch your words."

"I'm so sorry about all that," admitted Pip. "I know my temper is a problem, but I love you guys. All of you. Especially you, Patrick. I'll get help. I already am, actually. After I attacked Leo, I went to see someone, and I'm getting guidance for my anger issues. I wish I was different, and I'll try, I promise. Forgive me?"

"How can I?" asked Patrick. "You abused me. You hit me. How can I ever trust you? That's not how relationships are meant to be. Ever."

"I know. I understand we'll never be a couple again, but please let me try to make amends so we can be friends? Please?"

"Maybe," grunted Patrick, and that seemed to mollify Pip.

"But all these issues are just how life is for most of us. There are arguments, disagreements, maybe not violent ones, but it happens. No, there's something else, and it pushed Aggie and Kent over the edge. Right?" I asked, turning to the couple.

"Wrong," said Aggie. Her features softened and a sly smile appeared then vanished before she looked like a kind lady who wouldn't hurt a fly. "You all know me. I'm not violent. I would never, ever do this."

"We know," said Ollie. "Max, I appreciate you helping out, but this has gone too far. I think it's time you left, and I regret having to say this, but I don't want to see you again."

"Ollie, you're a kind man, that's obvious, but Patrick's right. You have secrets of your own. He couldn't figure it out, but I have."

"I... I don't know what you mean," he stammered, his cheeks pinpoints of red that he hid by playing with his helmet.

"You've been scared to admit the truth, haven't you? There's no shame in it. Patrick obviously picked up on something but didn't know what, so got a strange feeling about you."

"This is nonsense! Like I said, I think it's time you left."

"What is it?" asked Erin. "What has Ollie done?"

"Ollie hasn't done anything," I said. "He was just afraid."

"Afraid?"

"Of being found out."

"Okay, I admit it!" declared Ollie, stepping forward. "I'm broke. Utterly broke. I'm stressed beyond belief, worried for my family's future, and all of yours, so when Patrick left it became too much. If things don't change soon, I'll lose my house and the business."

"That's what you were trying to hide?" asked Patrick softly. "Why didn't you say something? I would have stayed if I knew things were that bad."

"Because I was embarrassed, and I'm the boss. I didn't want you to worry about me, or about your jobs, and the ridiculous thing is that now Leo is dead, our customers are returning and saying they wish they'd never left. In a few months we'll probably be fine again, but it's been a terrible year and I was ashamed. I don't want to close the practice, and I don't want everyone to lose their jobs, but there was nothing I could do."

"I'll come back. If you'll have me?" said Patrick.

"You will? Really?"

"Yes. I hate it at that place. It was a terrible decision and I regretted it instantly. I'll return and we'll make it the best practice in Wales. If that's okay with Pip too?"

"Yes, that would be amazing. Please come back. And please forgive me."

"So that leaves Aggie and Kent," I said, keeping my face serious as I hid my pleasure at Ollie admitting the truth and the practice seemingly being saved from closing and leaving the faceless corporation with their high prices in charge of everyone's animals.

We turned to the couple who were now isolated from the rest of us and gripping each other's hands tightly.

"We did nothing," insisted Aggie. "We never would. Why would you think such a thing?"

"It's obvious," I said. "The rubber dog toy."

The group exchanged shrugs and frowns, but I caught the glance Aggie gave Kent and pushed past everyone before they blocked me from confronting the couple.

Anxıous ducked between Erin's legs and sat between me and the pair, then barked a warning.

"Don't let his size fool you. He'll go after you if you try to run." I bent to Anxious and whispered, "Chase if they run."

He cocked his head, looked from me to them, then growled, deep and menacing.

Kent laughed and said, "He's smaller than my grandson's teddy. You think I'm worried about a little Jack Russell?"

"Kent, stop being mean. Anxious is a lovely dog and wouldn't hurt us, would you, boy?" cooed Aggie.

Anxious growled and his hackles rose.

"Max, that's enough!" ordered Ollie. "This has gone on too long. Explain yourself, right now, then leave. You're upsetting everyone."

I took a deep breath, composed myself, then let it all out. "Aggie put the rubber dog toy in her own mouth the moment the smoke clouded the room because she knew she'd be found out otherwise. She's got one volume, very loud, and she knew she'd end up saying something and give herself away. It also made it look like she was attacked too. She wasn't. Kent threw in the smoke grenades, Aggie put the toy in her mouth, then they both attacked the owners and Kent took the animals in the confusion while Aggie stabbed Riley."

"That's just not true," snapped Aggie, bristling at the accusation.

"There's more. I told you all I saw Kent arguing with Leo, and it turns out he'd had issues with Riley as well. They argued about the spot behind the houses the same as Kent, Leo, and Aggie did. I spoke to a neighbour today, and it's been going on for months. Ever since Leo began working in town and moved into the house by Aggie and Kent, there's been an issue over the parking. Riley used to park there, too, sometimes, and they all had run-ins. That's what this is all about."

"An argument over a parking space?" asked Ollie. "This is about someone who has it in for vets and wanted to sell the animals, surely? Max, you're acting nuts."

"He's right," said Erin. "Aggie complained to me all the time about Riley and Leo taking the spot, but I didn't think anything of it. I chatted with a neighbour ages ago and she said they almost came to blows, but, Max, that's not a reason to murder two people. I put it down to local gossip, nothing more. That's all it was."

"It's a valid reason if it's your livelihood and you keep getting blocked in, or are getting on in years and have to keep hauling your gear back and forth to the van when it could be almost right outside your back garden."

"This is stupid," said Kent with a scowl at me. "Nobody kills over a parking spot."

"You had it all planned out," I continued. "You'd get rid of Riley, take the animals to make some decent money, and then murder Leo. You knew it would look like a business dispute and suspicion would fall on Ollie, or at the very least on a gang of animal smugglers, but the truth is much more mundane, isn't it? You're both vitriolic, mean, nasty, vindictive people who don't like anyone getting the better of you. I looked up your crimes, Kent, from all those years ago, and one thing puzzled me about it all. Who helped you? How did you manage to seemingly be in two places at once? You never gave up your accomplice, and now we know why. Because it was your wife, and you'd never let her go to jail. Well, game's up, and this time you'll both go to prison. Aggie for murdering Riley, Kent for killing Leo. You shouldn't have attacked me last night, Kent. Your dodgy knee isn't from your younger days, it's because I kicked you early this morning. You'll both serve years for this. Decades, most likely."

"Never!" shouted Aggie in a panic. "You can't prove anything. Where's your evidence, eh?" she said with a sneer that turned into a mean smile, revealing her true nature.

"Nobody will ever believe you. There's no proof and it's all utterly ridiculous."

"You're forgetting one thing," I said calmly, when inside I was raging and almost quaking with adrenaline and nerves.

"And what's that?" asked Kent as a strange silence descended over the group now everyone realised I might be telling the truth.

"Remember the display in the waiting room? With all the treats and medications, the toys and the cute soft dogs with the funny eyes?"

"What about them?" asked Kent warily.

"Some of them were doggie cams, Kent. They are for pet owners to keep an eye on their animals. You set them up and they are motion activated. They can be linked to your phone, but record too. Well, I popped in with Erin earlier, and while she was busy giving the dogs some exercise I had a look at the smoke-damaged things Ollie had stored in the back room. One of them was active. It filmed everything. Sure, there was a lot of smoke, but it was trained on the reception area. It captured Aggie putting the dog toy in her mouth, and there was enough of a view, because, remember night-vision is part of the camera, to capture Aggie clearly enough killing Riley."

Everyone gasped. Erin shot me a confused look, but I just nodded, and Kent spun to his wife.

"You stupid woman! How could you be so daft? Now we'll go away for years. For life, most likely. And we nearly got away with it."

"Quiet, you fool! He made that up. There are no doggie cameras," spat Aggie, her face writhing in indecision and fear as her eyes darted.

"You lied?" asked Kent. "You tricked me?"

"I did. But now we know the truth."

At that moment, Dai and another man came careening towards us on their quad bikes and skidded to a stop. Both dismounted right beside us, and Dai asked, "Hey, what are you all doing? Time's up, and we have another group waiting to go. What's going on?"

Kent grabbed Aggie by the arm and shoved Dai aside then almost flung Aggie onto the quad, jumped in front of her, and revved the throttle then turned in a sharp circle and roared away.

"Stop him!" shouted Ollie.

"What's happening here? He can't do that!" shouted Dai.

"No time to explain. I need to borrow the other one," I shouted, then ran to the quad. Anxious jumped into the basket on the rear, and I spun the handles to give chase. I felt something behind me and turned to find Erin sitting there, grinning.

"No way am I missing out on this," she insisted, then wrapped her hands around my waist.

With no time to argue, I said, "Hold on tight," then kicked up dirt as I sped after Kent and Aggie, knowing we wouldn't stand a chance if we used Vee. Adorable, quirky, and fun she might be, but fast she was not.

Kent and Aggie were lost to a cloud of dust as they sped for the exit, so I pulled my goggles down, only now realising we were all still wearing our paint-spattered paintball gear. I fished out Anxious' goggles from my pocket and reached behind as I turned to Erin and said, "Can you put these on Anxious? Just in case."

"In case of what?"

"I honestly don't know," I admitted.

Erin explained to Anxious what she was about to do, and he obviously let her as when I glanced behind they both had their goggles in place, looking like they were about to go into battle, but for real this time. Maybe we all were.

"Max, this is madness. Aggie and Kent really did it? How were you so sure?"

"Because of the dog toy. I knew there was something I was overlooking. Something obvious. Why would anyone do that to Aggie? But she knew she'd end up shouting out, or talking, or doing something that might have given her position away, so she used the dog toy."

"But all for a parking spot? No way?"

"Yes, for a parking spot. After you left earlier, I questioned the neighbours. They all spoke about the arguing over it, and at first I thought nothing of it, but then I looked into Kent's past and what he'd done. It was just spite. And I got to thinking about Aggie's involvement, and how she was his alibi this time, but maybe she was involved then too. It made sense."

"It's still a big leap from arguing over parking to murder."

"Not really. They're spiteful people, and Aggie hated Leo like so many others. She didn't want to lose her job. My guess is, she suspected Ollie had money problems and feared she'd be out of work. It's not easy to get a new position when you're in your sixties. So why not eliminate Leo and ensure her job was safe, and get the parking spot too?"

"Wow, you're so smart. But come on, even that's still not much to cause someone to commit murder. What else?"

"Nothing," I admitted. "Just what my gut was telling me. Once I heard about the parking issue, the rest slotted into place."

"What if you'd been wrong?"

"But I wasn't, was I?" I grinned, turning to her. "Now, can you call the police? I think we're going to need them."

Erin made the call while I exited the paintball forest and spied Kent and Aggie taking a turn up ahead that led back to town. Where were they going? What was the plan here?

Time to find out. I thumbed the throttle and we rocketed after them, Anxious barking with excitement from the rear.

Chapter 20

We tore through the lanes, Kent clearly unhinged as he hurtled across junctions, ignoring the roadworks and temporary traffic lights no matter what colour they were or what was approaching.

I took a more sensible approach. Remaining alive was much more important than catching them first. Erin pushed me repeatedly to drive faster and run the red lights, but I refused—if anything happened to her or Anxious I would be to blame.

It made little difference anyway, as I throttled it and we surged forward to find the road blocked by a tractor hauling a large flatbed. Kent weaved side-to-side, trying to find an opening, and glanced over his shoulder. When he spied us, he spoke to Aggie, who pounded on his shoulder, presumably telling him to get past.

They had most likely assumed they could make it home and switch vehicles, maybe grab a few things before they were caught, but now the pair were out of luck and out of time. The tractor pulled into a lay-by to let traffic pass, something I had always been pleased to see as it showed real thought for other drivers, and Kent floored it. He raced towards town like a thing possessed, whilst I drove as fast as I could without risking anything, certain they'd be stopped one way or another soon enough.

With the roar of the engine drowning out all other sound, and the wind whipping at my hair and clothes, I was pleased I had the goggles so my eyes didn't tear up, and wiped at a spot of blue paint to improve my vision.

Erin tapped me on the shoulder and pointed to the right as she hollered, "There they are."

"Where are they going?" I shouted over my shoulder.

"No idea. The wrong way, by the looks of it. This is so much fun!"

"Fun? I'm terrified," I screamed against the wind as my hair slapped into my mouth and my beard felt like it was being torn from my face.

I took the turn to follow them, and glanced to the left to find that the main road through town was blocked, unsurprisingly for overnight roadworks, of which there was no sign. Kent had no choice but to go down the hill with the castle on the right.

The obscene decline would be extremely hairy on the quad bikes, and I braced myself for the descent, but up ahead the road was filling with smoke as the exhaust from Kent's quad belched. Suddenly, there was an almighty bang and a screech of brakes as the quad bumped into the empty car park, toppled precariously, righted, then skidded sideways towards the wall protecting people from the dry moat.

The quad slammed sideways into ancient stone with a crunch of metal and plastic. Kent and Aggie screamed as they sailed over the wall and were gone.

Slowing carefully, I parked beside the wall and Anxious slipped onto the stone and began to bark. Erin and I untangled ourselves from each other as she was now gripping around my neck with one arm and had wrapped her other around me awkwardly, then dismounted and rushed over as the crumpled quad spluttered before the engine cut out with a dull clang.

"There they are!" Erin pointed at the two figures hobbling across the moat then clambering over the rocks, both seemingly uninjured thanks to the tumble onto soft, spongy grass. Kent hauled Aggie up the steepest section before they disappeared into the castle remains and were lost from sight.

"Can you get out over the other side?" I asked, panting.

"Yes, you can walk around, but there's also a path down onto the road. We should go after them."

"Just be careful. There's no need to take any risks. They aren't exactly sprightly, and where can they go anyway?"

"I know, but if they disappear, they might not be found again. Kent might steal a car. Come on." Erin hopped over the wall, slid down the embankment, then raced across the moat.

With a sigh, I climbed over, dropped onto my bum, then bounced over the rough ground to join her while Anxious yipped with excitement beside me.

"Go find them, Anxious," I encouraged as he sat, waiting for instructions.

He tapped his goggles, shook himself out so his paint-covered tiny tactical vest rode high up his neck, then turned and gave chase, sniffing as he followed their trail like he was hunting rabbits.

"Think you can make it up the other side?" asked Erin with a grin, her face flushed and forehead sweaty.

"If they got up, then I certainly can. Let's go."

Together, we clambered up the side of the moat, gripping sections of rock for purchase, then ducked between the teetering walls into the castle grounds.

It was eerie without the tourists, and I shivered as I pictured ghosts of the past walking through me. The walls cast long shadows across the well-trampled grass, hardly any sunlight here now save for a few shafts beaming through the decaying, ancient windows.

Where were they?

We hurried to the far side of the grounds and eased through a crack until we were outside the castle and looking out to the sand dunes and the still sea beyond. The path was clear, so either they were faster than we'd anticipated or they were hiding, hoping they'd given us the slip.

"Anxious, where are they?" I asked him.

He turned back into the castle and barked, so we followed. I cursed myself for not paying enough attention to him in the first place as he raced over to the turret then sat and stared at the dark entrance to the high walls.

"They must have gone up," I whispered to Erin.

"Or they're waiting to ambush us just inside with rocks," she said, stepping back.

"Good thinking. Let's see if we can spot them from the other side."

We hurried away, keeping close to the walls, hoping to spy them on the parapet, when suddenly I felt a thwack on my head, then another, then another. Next thing I knew, I was blind as blue paint splatted onto my goggles and I got a taste of the stuff.

"They've still got their guns and plenty of ammunition!" I warned as I ducked low.

"Where are they?" squealed Erin, before she staggered back under a vicious onslaught of blue gunge that covered her helmet and goggles.

"Up there." I pointed, catching sight of them both crouched in a corner by the railings, guns centred on us.

"Right, that does it!" Erin whipped a paintball pistol from her waistband and filled the magazine, then grinned manically.

"Don't suppose you have a spare?" I sighed wistfully.

"A lady always comes prepared," she said, then pulled out another, loaded it, and handed it to me.

"Where'd that come from? Did you have these earlier?"

"Like you discovered, I'm a big paintball fan and have my own weapons. Quality ones, not the junk they let people use in the woods. These are properly accurate and pretty dangerous, so be careful. Don't fire at anyone's face, but go for their legs. It'll slow the buggers down and confuse them, if nothing else."

"Okay, then let's do this," I cheered, getting carried away by the rush I was having. It wasn't quite the SAS, but I still felt like a real soldier now I held a rather grubby paintball gun in my hands.

Keeping low, we made a dash for it across the open ground with Anxious leading the way. He was the first to receive enemy fire, and howled as a ball exploded on his right flank, but he was a trooper and it hardly slowed him, and he made it to the far wall with just a few more blue blobs on his tactical vest and goggles.

Erin and I fared much worse, our heads plastered in paint by the time we made it, so we took a moment to clean Anxious and each other up, then Erin covered me from the doorway as I entered the turret, gun held in front and gripped tightly in one hand, the other supporting my wrist like I'd seen on the TV.

"Clear," I couldn't help shouting, truly immersed in the moment now.

Erin danced inside, and she covered me again, two steps behind, as we surged up the spiralling stairs. At the exit, I paused, scanned for hostiles, then jumped out and crouched before Erin joined me. Anxious crawled on his belly to make himself less of a target, deep in military-mode.

Together, we eased along the narrow parapet, mindful of how long the drop was, bent over to ensure we didn't go tumbling over the side. Anxious remained on his tummy, which slowed him down, but at least he didn't have to look at how far he might fall.

Aggie and Kent were huddled together at the end of the walkway, nowhere to go, looking angry, dejected, and obstinate to the very end.

"Nobody move!" shouted Erin, more caught up in the game of cops and robbers than me, as she trained her paintball gun on them then fired off two warning shots at the wall behind.

Aggie squealed, Kent hid his face behind his hands, and Anxious, suddenly on his feet, ran forward, sat in front of them, and barked a warning.

"I don't think they're going anywhere now," I told Erin, putting a hand to the gun so she'd lower it.

She turned to me, nodded, then stashed the weapon. I gave her mine, then we approached.

"What did you think you were doing?" I asked, genuinely interested.

"We didn't know where else to go. The road was closed. We thought we could get down the path, but my leg's playing up. That's your fault!" hissed Kent. "Aggie wouldn't go without me, so we thought we'd have one last look at the castle. We do love it."

"We do. It's our favourite place," agreed Aggie. "We've been here so many times before. It's special. We love the stone walls."

"There'll be plenty of walls to stare at where you're going," grunted Erin. She turned to me, beaming, and asked, "That was a good line, right? Like in a movie."

I stared at her, then Anxious, then Aggie and Kent, all of us in paint-covered, fake tactical gear, marks on our faces from the goggles, oversized helmets, and I laughed. I just laughed. I couldn't help myself. It was so ridiculous, and I was so hyped from the chase, that I just saw the funny side of it.

Soon, Erin was bent double, Anxious was howling, and Aggie and Kent just sat there, beaten, gawping at us in confusion.

Our mirth died soon enough, as this was a serious matter. As we approached, sirens grew closer, then the castle grounds were awash with police officers, detectives, and the crew from paintball.

"Time to go," I said, keeping my distance. "There's nowhere to run now."

"Can't run anyway with my leg giving me trouble," grumbled Kent like this was just a minor inconvenience, not the end of their life as they knew it.

I leaned over the railing and called down, "We're up here," then Erin and I retreated to the stairwell while Anxious remained keeping guard.

I don't think he needed to have bothered, but after the fine job he'd done I didn't want to spoil the end for him.

When the police officers and detectives arrived, we explained what had happened and what Aggie and Kent had admitted to, and after promising to remain below we were allowed to descend the stairs and join the others.

Everyone was pleased to see us, amazed at what had happened and the revelations, but Ollie still found it hard to believe the truth. I guess we all did to some extent.

"It just can't be true," he insisted. "Over parking?"

"That's what it seems to be. I'm assuming there are money issues, and Aggie must have been desperate to keep her job. Ollie, she most likely discovered the problems you were facing and worried about her position, so took this opportunity to ensure you remained open for business and eliminate her problems too. I know it's incredulous, but trust me, after the things I've been involved in lately, nothing would surprise me. People kill for all manner of reasons, and some of them are downright ridiculous."

"I know what people are capable of, but this is Aggie. Loud, crotchety, but always loyal Aggie."

"And she was loyal to the last," I said. "She even committed murder to keep your place open and keep her job."

"Plus the parking," said Erin. "Don't forget the parking."

"Nobody will ever forget that," I said.

We turned to watch the police bring a very subdued Aggie and Kent through the turret, then cuffed them before they were led across the grass. We followed behind, although I'm not sure why. Someone must have been called because the bridge was open and lights were on in the visitor centre, so nobody had to use the moat.

The bridge was beautiful with the mellow lighting as the sun sank lower, and Anxious led the way like a proud parent, never once pausing as he crossed the bridge with his head held high, looking like a miniature sniper in his combat gear.

Aggie and Kent were loaded into a van in the car park, then taken away, leaving us with the detectives and several officers. After speaking to them again, we promised to go to the station to give statements, so it would be a long evening.

Once they left, the paintball guys turned up looking for their quad bikes. After hearty apologies and a lot of questions to answer, they left, too, until it was just the vet crowd plus Cindy. I was pleased to see she was standing beside Rhys and they were both smiling as they whispered to each other. Seemed like at least the day had been a success for two people.

I felt no smug sense of satisfaction at seeing this through, just relief that it was over and nobody else would be harmed.

"Time to give your statements, if you don't mind," said an officer. "Does anyone need a lift?"

After arranging transport, we converged on the police station to give our side of what was a very sorry, and very deadly, story.

Chapter 21

"Max, you weren't going to leave without saying goodbye, were you?" asked Erin, hands on her hips, a tight smile on her face.

"As if," I grinned. "Anxious would never let me do that, would you?"

Anxious barked, then raced over to Erin and rubbed against her legs until he got a well-deserved stroke and a scratch behind the ears.

"That's good," laughed Erin as Anxious wandered off and took up position underneath Vee as the sun rose and the heat intensified.

"Thanks for all your help over the last few days. It's been great hanging out, and lovely to meet you, Erin."

"Max, the pleasure's been all mine. We would have been in a right mess otherwise. You saved the practice, caught the killers, and even acted as matchmaker."

"They've really hit it off, haven't they?"

"They sure have," scowled Erin. "It's gross. Rhys and Cindy are like two teenagers. Always holding hands, whispering to each other and laughing, and don't even get me started on what they get up to on the sofa while I'm trying to watch TV."

"Hey, it's been good for them both. They need each other. Rhys had already sworn off the booze, and he's stuck to it these last few days, which is great. I think he'll stay sober."

"Me too. He's like a different person after he admitted what he'd done to the police. And he's in the clear. No record, no fine or anything. Just a stern warning. He's promised to go straight from now on."

"You should be proud of him."

"I am. Thanks again, Max. I know Ollie is beyond relieved, although he still can't accept Aggie did this. None of us can. She was always loud and obstinate, but murder? It's crazy."

"But now we all know her and Kent had real money issues and that most likely was the real motive. She worked in the bar and the vets, he did whatever he could to earn money, even with his health issues, but like the police told us, they uncovered gambling debts from online gaming that they were both addicted to and they saw no way out. When people are that stressed, they don't think straight, and they just panicked."

"Some panic! They killed two people. She could have come to me."

"Aggie's a proud woman and wouldn't ever do that. You know how she is."

"I thought I did. But you're right, she would never ask for help. So, what's next?" Erin moved closer, so close I could smell her perfume, and her voice lowered and softened. "You can always stay," she almost purred, an eyebrow raised.

"That's a very tempting offer, but you know my position."

"Max, I'm just messing with you," she giggled, slapping me on the back. "I would never try to steal another woman's man, even if she is nuts for not being here with you."

"You know it's complicated. But give it time and it will work out."

"You know what? I'm sure you're right. You're a great guy and Min's a lucky woman. But from what I know of her, you're a lucky man too."

"You have no idea. Truly, you don't. Erin, I put her through hell and I'm lucky she even wants to talk to me, let alone give me a second chance. I'm doing my best to change, but it's difficult."

"You're doing great, Max, just great. Don't be so hard on yourself."

"Thank you. So, what's next for you?"

"Work, and not a lot else," she shrugged. "Ollie's all excited because the business has picked up, and it seems like the other practice is staying shut as they don't think there's enough profit in this area. They want the big bucks, whereas Ollie just wants to earn a decent living and keep us all employed."

"That's great. He's a good guy, and I'm glad it worked out between him and Patrick."

"See, I was right about that. It was just a misunderstanding." Erin grinned and couldn't hide her smugness.

"You were right," I admitted. "But so was Patrick. He knew something was up, but he was wrong about what it was. Hey, did you ever discover where Kent got all the gear from to attack the clinic?"

"No idea, but people talk, and word is that he's a bit of an army nut. Might have had stuff knocking around and just bought the smoke grenades from the guys at paintball. Who knows? It doesn't matter. The main thing is they tracked down all the animals and returned them to their rightful homes. Aggie was more upset about doing that than the killing. The first thing she confessed to was selling them to dodgy friends of Kent, and the police uncovered quite a large operation, didn't they?"

"They sure did. I can't believe people would stoop that low. Stealing animals and selling them on the black market, then they end up with a poor family who know nothing about their history. It's awful."

"But now they're back, and everyone's safe. Thanks once again, Max. You're a real sweetheart." Erin stood on tiptoe and planted a kiss on my cheek, then in her usual style she wandered back up the garden and waved over her shoulder.

"I'll miss her," I sighed, watching her enter the house.

Anxious barked his agreement, then sat, head cocked, eyes on my pocket.

"Just one, then we need to get going," I laughed, fishing out a biscuit that he took gently then returned to his campervan den.

The sun shelter and outdoor kitchen were all packed up, the water was topped up in the campervan, bed folded away, everything stored in its rightful place, and there was nothing to do but stow my camping chair and hit the road.

But I couldn't resist one more sit before we left. We were in no hurry. The music festival didn't open for another five days, so we'd make a few short stops on the way to England, waving a sorry farewell to Wales as we went. But we'd be back, there was no doubt about that. After all, our home really was wherever we lay our heads.

Despite everything that had happened, I couldn't help thinking about the note I'd found. HELP ME. What did it mean? Did it mean anything at all? Was there anything I could do to find out? No, it was ancient history, right?

Anxious launched into my lap and settled, so I remained there for a while as he snored. There was no hurry. The one thing I wasn't short of was time.

The End

But it isn't really! Read on for another stunning one-pot recipe and an update about what to expect next for Max and Anxious as their vanlife adventure continues in **A Festival of Fear**! Music, food, performing arts, and one mighty mystery sees Max, Anxious, and maybe a few surprise guests all embroiled in a truly grisly murder mystery of meaty proportions. Don't miss it!

But first, let's cook...

Recipe

Slow Cooked Pork, Cider, & Sage Hotpot

Pork and apple is always a beautiful pairing. Throw in some aromatic sage and crispy potatoes and you have a perfect pork supper.

This recipe will feed four with plenty of leftovers (hopefully).

I've suggested finishing this in the oven, but of course you could make like Max and cook it on an open fire with the Dutch Oven lid covered in hot coals for much the same effect. It's a perfect excuse to spend some time outdoors, and who doesn't love a fire?

If you're feeling decadent you can add cream (single or sour would work), and of course add more veggies with the leeks for something lighter and no less tasty.

Ingredients

- Season the pork with salt and pepper and put the oil over a medium high heat.
- Diced pork (shoulder is ideal) – around 1kg / 2lb
- Flour – 2 tbsp
- Rapeseed or sunflower oil – 2 tbsp
- Butter – a decent knob, cubed
- Leeks – 4 roughly chopped into large coins.
- Four garlic cloves, crushed
- Plain flour – 3 tbsp
- Dry cider – 500ml / 1pt
- Chicken or vegetable stock - 500ml / 1pt
- Single cream – 175ml / 0.75 cups

- Seasoning - salt, pepper, a couple of bay leaves, and a small bunch of sage leaves chopped
- Waxy potatoes sliced thickly into large coins (500g / 1lb)

Method

You will need a large casserole/Dutch Oven or similar with a well fitting lid.

- Season the pork with salt and pepper and put the oil over a medium high heat.
- In batches you need to fry the pork to colour lightly without overloading the pot.
- Once the pork is all golden, add the leeks to your pot and turn the heat down to medium. You'll want to cook the leeks slowly for ten minutes, to soften without colouring. Be sure to scrape up all the gnarly bits of porky goodness from the base of the pot. Crispy bits are always the best!
- The moment they look nice and squidgy, add the garlic, flour, and bay leaves. Give it a good stir.
- Now pop in the cider a little at a time. You'll want to stir vigorously to stop the flour forming any lumps.
- Now everything is incorporated, add the stock, sage, and pork. Bring it all to a boil, then turn down and simmer for around 90 minutes. You'll need a lid placed at a suitably jaunty angle to stop all the liquid disappearing.
- When the time's up, pop the oven on at 200C / 400F. While the oven gets up to temperature, turn the heat up and take the lid off your casserole so the sauce can reduce down a little.

- When the oven is ready, remove the pot from the heat. Now stir in the cream (if using) and then top with layers of sliced potato. Be sure to sprinkle a little extra salt on top, along with the cubes of butter.
- Pop the pot in the oven, uncovered, and bake for another 1-1½ hrs until the potatoes are both soft within, and golden outside.

That's it! You should have fall apart, melt-in-the-mouth pork topped with crispy, fluffy potatoes. Yum!

As for this feeding four, with leftovers... I'll leave that up to you. Might want to loosen that belt!

From the Author

Max certainly had a lot to contend with this time, and so did poor Anxious. He's so brave, and coped so well with being fixed-up by THE DOCTOR! I'm very proud of him. In all seriousness, I know how scary going to the vets can be for many animals. Some love it, others not so much. Over the years, we've had a real mixture of dogs, each with their own opinion on whether a visit is justified (mostly they think not), but just like people, we have to look after each other.

Max and Min's relationship continues to occupy his waking thoughts, and his dreams, but I think they're both handling it very well. Sometimes it's really tough being a grown-up. And we thought we had it hard when we were kids!

What's next for Max and Anxious? Time to find out...

Continue Max's Campervan Case Files in A Festival of Fear! It gets gnarly, as Erin would say. But at least there's festival food, an occasional pint, and some rocking music. Plus a murder, of course.

Be sure to stay updated about new releases and fan sales. You'll hear about them first. No spam, just book updates at www.authortylerrhodes.com

You can also follow me on Amazon www.amazon.com/stores/author/B0BN6T2VQ5

Connect with me on Facebook www.facebook.com/authortylerrhodes/

Printed in Great Britain
by Amazon